PENGUIN BOOKS

A CHRISTMAS BLIZZARD

Garrison Keillor is the author of the Lake Wobegon novels, most recently *Pilgrims: A Lake Wobegon Romance,* and *77 Love Sonnets* and the creator of *A Prairie Home Companion.*

GARRISON KEILLOR

A Christmas Blizzard

PENGUIN BOOKS

PENGUIN BOOKS
Published by the Penguin Group
Penguin Group (USA) Inc., 375 Hudson Street, New York, New York 10014, U.S.A.
Penguin Group (Canada), 90 Eglinton Avenue East, Suite 700, Toronto,
Ontario, Canada M4P 2Y3 (a division of Pearson Penguin Canada Inc.)
Penguin Books Ltd, 80 Strand, London WC2R 0RL, England
Penguin Ireland, 25 St Stephen's Green, Dublin 2, Ireland (a division of Penguin Books Ltd)
Penguin Group (Australia), 250 Camberwell Road, Camberwell,
Victoria 3124, Australia (a division of Pearson Australia Group Pty Ltd)
Penguin Books India Pvt Ltd, 11 Community Centre,
Panchsheel Park, New Delhi – 110 017, India
Penguin Group (NZ), 67 Apollo Drive, Rosedale, Auckland 0632,
New Zealand (a division of Pearson New Zealand Ltd)
Penguin Books (South Africa) (Pty) Ltd, 24 Sturdee Avenue,
Rosebank, Johannesburg 2196, South Africa

Penguin Books Ltd, Registered Offices: 80 Strand, London WC2R 0RL, England

First published in the United States of America by Viking Penguin,
a member of Penguin Group (USA) Inc. 2009
Published in Penguin Books 2011

9 10 8

Copyright © Garrison Keillor, 2009, 2011
All rights reserved

Publisher's Note
This is a work of fiction. Names, characters, places, and incidents either are the product
of the author's imagination or are used fictitiously, and any resemblance to actual persons,
living or dead, business establishments, events, or locales is entirely coincidental.

THE LIBRARY OF CONGRESS HAS CATALOGED THE HARDCOVER EDITION AS FOLLOWS:
Keillor, Garrison.
A Christmas blizzard / Garrison Keillor.
p. cm.
ISBN 978-0-670-02136-9 (hc.)
ISBN 978-0-14-311988-3 (pbk.)
1. Christmas stories.   2. Man-woman relationships—Fiction.
3. Chicago (Ill.)—Fiction   I. Title.
PS3561.E3755C48 2009
813'.54—dc22   2009035850

Printed in the United States of America
Set in Aldus   Design by Daniel Lagin

A Christmas Blizzard

1. James Sparrow awakens too early and is besieged by the mean Christmas blues

I t was an old familiar nightmare, the one about screechy men in black hoods chasing him through tall razor grass toward the precipice overlooking jagged rocks and great bilious greenish waves rolling and crashing in the vast abyss where sharks with chainsaw teeth waited to chew him to ribbons and great black buzzards soared and screeched, and there he was running barefoot and his pajama bottoms falling down and heart pounding as if to burst and he unable to cry out for help and then Mr. Sparrow woke up in the darkness of his condo in south Minneapolis to a song emanating from somewhere close to the bed—

When he plays his drum, pa-rum-pum-pum-pum,
Let's break his thumbs

He thought maybe it was part of the dream, the Christmas carol he loathed most of all, the loathsomest song of the dreadful Yuletide season, that godawful month (heck, two months! maybe three) of relentless, regimented, joyless joy, and he lay waiting for the men to throw him over the cliff, but they had evaporated, and only the loathsome song remained:

I played my drum for Him, pa-rum-pum-pum-pum
He told me, Beat it, Jim, pa-rum-pum-pum-pum

It was dark except for a faint glow from the bathroom. Mrs. Sparrow lay asleep next to him in their double bed in the tiny bedroom of Unit F in the Middlesex Arms condominium complex. It was a former linseed oil factory that a dishonest developer had made into apartments and sold to gullible buyers. Dazzled by the ornate Art Deco lobby, they paid a fortune for rather cramped one-bedrooms with temperamental plumbing and tissue-paper walls and ill-fitted windows. In this December cold snap, the bedroom was freezing. He edged closer to Mrs. Sparrow, a good warm wife. It was December 22. In two days, the red-green monster of Christmas would descend.

The World's Longest and Unhappiest Holiday. Mrs. Sparrow adored Christmas, and Mr. Sparrow dreaded it. It gave him a bad case of the yips. The brass quintets tootling "God Rest Ye Merry, Gentlemen" on street corners and the sugarplum fairies twirling in the windows of Macy's, and inside, between Cosmetics and Housewares, a pianist plowing through the little town of Bethlehem like a backhoe digging a ditch. It was ubiquitous, inescapable, the jingle-jangle, the ho-ho-ho, the smell of pine, the bullying ads, and the guilt—the nagging thought that you had not bought gifts for all the people you should have and the gifts you had bought were not nice enough and you were not joyful, as you should be, seeing as God had sent His Son to earth for your redemption—you, wretched sinner that you are, should be dancing for joy, and instead you feel crappy. You wish you could drive Christmas away, this whole dark fog of nostalgia and disappointment.

Why could they not use the money Mrs. Sparrow had inherited at the death of her dad to fly to Hawaii, *pa-rum-pum-pum-pum*, and lounge on the beach at that lovely resort at Kuhikuhikapapa'u'maumau, where they had spent their honeymoon four years ago? Sometimes, when a man is in the depths of misery, a good vacation is a wise investment. Yes, he understood that they were in bad shape financially. The real estate market was in the toilet. The condo, heavily mortgaged, was worth about half of what they had paid for it, and they were pouring money into a rat hole. And Mr. Sparrow was very likely on the verge of losing his job. (He had not shared this information with his wife.) He was a communications specialist at Coyote Corp., which made an energy drink from ionized chlorophyll from coyote grass, and which was struggling in the wake of lawsuits by consumers who had suffered violent intestinal upsets. The owner of Coyote, Billy Jack Morosco, had retreated to his penthouse on the fifty-fifth floor of the Federated Mutual Tower to brood and conduct a séance with his advisors, and the axe was expected to fall soon after Christmas, and Mr. Sparrow expected to be handed his hat and pushed out the door.

Mr. Sparrow did not use Coyote himself, but he knew all about it. Coyote grass is a broad-stemmed plant devoured by coyotes during mating season, and the drink gives a person high energy and focus, inducing a manic state, enabling you to thrive on just three hours of sleep a night for months at a time. A greenish liquid, it was a word-of-mouth phenomenon in America's managerial ranks in the late 1990s. Millions of people knew about it—a few drops in your coffee and you were a monster of superhuman productivity and able to handle the avalanche of work that fell on middle managers beset by corporate cutbacks and mergers. Middle managers in their forties who felt antiquated by the hyperspeed of technological change and the new lingo that came with it. It was rocket fuel. You took home a briefcase bulging with work and labored late into the night and napped for a few hours and awoke before dawn feeling fresh and ambitious and showed up at the 7:00 a.m. meeting full of brilliance and you stunned the younger staff with a list of Large New Ideas and you maintained a killer pace all day, skipping lunch, and all around you, people marveled at your productivity and top management said, *What would we ever do without Perkins?* and you never never never complained about the workload, though your spouse and children did, but you ignored their sullen resentment and mounted your great steed and galloped every day back into battle. All thanks to a grass that coyotes ate to give them stamina to flirt and howl at the moon. The Sioux warriors who ate Custer's lunch at the Little Big Horn were tanked up on coyote grass.

"Oh darling Joyce. Oh Joyce, my love, let's away to the warm Pacific and float in the star-spangled sea," he had said to his wife one week ago. "Darling, the condo—" she said. He groaned. "Maybe you only need a sunlamp," she said. He groaned again. "Darling, we have to be reasonable," she said. She was the practical one who kept track of finances. Reasonableness was the aspect of her character that he found most annoying, and also her great love of Christmas. She had graduated from St. Olaf College and sung in the famous St. Olaf Choir, whose annual Christmas concert in the Skoglund fieldhouse was so popular that the college scheduled sixteen of them—*sixteen! Sixteen Silent Nights, sixteen Det kimer nu til Julefests, sixteen Harks, sixteen Midnights Clear.* The fieldhouse was packed for each one, St. Olaf alumni jammed cheek by jowl and tears running down their cheeks as the famous choir sang "Beautiful Savior"—and of course Mrs. Sparrow insisted on taking him down to Northfield to attend a concert. "But we've done this before!" he said. It didn't matter. And then there was Christmas Eve among the pesky Episcopalians at St. Ansgar's.

Mrs. Sparrow grew up Lutheran in a little church in Wauwatosa, Wisconsin, whose congregation sang so beautifully a capella—"As with Gladness Men of Old" and "Hark! the Herald Angels Sing" and "The First Noel" and "What Child Is This?"—that TV crews came to film them every year, which made them uneasy, worried about the sin of Pride, as Lutherans are wont to do, but then they hired a hearing-impaired organist to torture them and to put unfamiliar hymns in the service—"He of Whom the Nations Sing" and "Let Now Our Voices Gladly Rise" and "That Which Doth Our Hearts Inspire" and "Come Ye, Thou, of Heaven Inspir'd"—to prevent beautiful singing. And the congregation was reduced to murmurs, in keeping with the Lutheran beatitude, "Blessed are the meek and those who do not stand out from the others"—and that was what drove Mrs. Sparrow into the arms of the Episcopalians, the big 10:30 p.m. candlelit Christmas Eve service that ended with "Silent Night" sung a capella, people kneeling in the pews, each with a slender lit taper, each weeping quietly for the memories of Christmases past and the dear departed and also for the Holy Infant, who came in sympathy for the sorrows of the suffering world. The service at St. Ansgar's was a high point in Mrs. Sparrow's year. Mr. Sparrow accompanied her, of course, and stood and knelt and sat and stood, as directed, and did the responsive readings, but with an eye on his wristwatch. And it irked him that they sang *every last verse* of "Silent Night" and then *hummed* a verse and then *sang the first verse over*, squeezing every last ounce of emotion from it. And then there was bad coffee afterward, in the undercroft, and a lot of chitchat with people he didn't know, who, like so many Episcos, had a burr up their butt about some good cause they wanted to enlist him in: the Drop-in Center for Troubled Teens, the Outreach to the Introspective, a well for a village in Uganda, an exchange program for vicars, or whatever. Pure misery.

Mr. Sparrow was a Republican, and the Episcopal Church was not, and Christmas seemed to him an occasion for hectoring sermons about the needs of the needy and ending war and achieving international understanding and so forth, which was not, to put it mildly, his worldview. He felt that you pretty much get what you deserve in life—the weak fall apart, the strong prevail—and anything you do to change the rules will only confuse the matter. Before he went to work for Coyote, he taught high school math for two years, and it was a simple fact that two-thirds of the kids didn't grasp math and didn't care, and there wasn't much you could do for them except point them toward work that didn't require math, like sweeping floors or flipping burgers. The principal was a horse-faced liberal named Bettye Davenport, who believed that he should be more inspiring to the slow and the lame. His job, as he saw it, was to open doors for the ambitious and talented so they could see how high they could soar. Math is for the few. It's not something you take up suddenly in your late teens thanks to some government program. The high school wanted him to manage a summer program in math enrichment for marginal students, using $200,000 in federal funds, and Mr. Sparrow balked. The principal was of the If-we-can-help-just-one-sinking-soul school of thinking. He was not. She got up in his face about it, and he quit. End of story.

O the snow and the cold, the bleakness of light, and the sheer horror of "The Little Drummer Boy" coming at you when you least expected it, *pa-rum-pum-pum-pum*, and the obligatory trip to St. Olaf, plus the guilt, et cetera, et cetera— but Mrs. Sparrow was a true devotee of Christmas. She attended *The Nutcracker* every year, one and maybe two *Messiah*s, and three *A Christmas Carol*s. She never tired of Scrooge's redemption. She thrilled to the Sugar Plum Fairy, she made fruitcake at home, she went around whistling "Adeste Fideles." Mr. Sparrow wished that the mice would carry Clara away and lock her in a dungeon and that the Hallelujah chorus could be embargoed for ten years and that Tiny Tim would learn a useful trade and quit blessing people. Mr. Charles Dickens had no idea of the juggernaut he

launched. Back when he wrote about Scrooge and the neb-
bishy Cratchits, Christmas was a one-day event, like Valen-
tine's Day or Memorial Day, and you did the thing on that
day and it was over, but his little book touched off a prairie fire of Christmas, and it spread out of control, and now
the good man would have been horrified to see the monster
he created. The incessant dinging of bells. The godawful music seeping out of cracks in ceilings like liquid gas. The forced
jollity of store clerks living in the hellish anguish of holiday
merchandising, clerks so stressed out it was a wonder one of
them didn't go berserk and kill somebody with a stapler. The
disappointment of gifts. A gift represents the giver's percep-
tion of you, and when you unwrap the brown plaid shirt,
white socks, and a bar of soap that smells like disinfectant
they gave you rather than, say, black silk undershorts and a
volume of Baudelaire, the message could not be clearer. And
the dreadful parties. Especially the office parties, where people who don't like one another stand around getting glassy-
eyed on Artillery punch and avoiding the big honchos trying
too hard to be kindly and cheery, vice presidents and managers who for the rest of the year are professional killers.

The Coyote Corp. put on painful Christmas parties,
where the 325 employees and their spouses gathered in a
great hangar of a hotel ballroom to eat prime rib, and Mr.
Morosco stood up and talked about the founding of the firm
in 1974, when he met an old drunk in a bar in Livingston,

Montana, who sold him the formula for a tonic for $250 and from that formula Mr. Morosco built a successful company. It was a story that most of them had heard many times before, and they sat through it and gave him a standing ovation, and then a gang of glittery Christmas elves pranced into the room and handed out bonus checks and everybody sang "We Wish You a Merry Christmas" and "For He's a Jolly Good Fellow" and rushed for the exits.

Mr. Sparrow's bonus this year was a measly four grand. A sign of trouble. He'd hoped for ten or fifteen grand.

He hoisted himself up on one elbow and gazed at her, his true love, in her cardigan sweater, soft purple pants, and red socks, her earbuds in place. He groped for the bedside lamp so he could find the radio that was playing the loathsome Christmas carol and knocked a book off the stack on the bedside table and also his eyedrops and he almost spilled a glass of juice. Mrs. Sparrow turned over but did not open her eyes. He put the glass to his lips and—*pfffffffeh!!!!!!!!!!*—cranberry juice! Cranberry juice. The taste of cranberry brought back unpleasant memories, the boredom of breast of turkey, the big yawn of yams, the pointlessness of pumpkin.

> *Said the shepherd to the little lamb,*
> *I have a gift to bring, pa-rum-pum-pum-pum*
> *A noose and scaffolding, pa-rum-pum-pum-pum.*

It was the digital clock radio playing the song. An iClock. You could access your bank account, activate a coffeemaker, download a newspaper, open up e-mail and have it read to you in a pleasant female voice. A marvelous device, playing Christmas music that made him faintly ill, and he didn't know how to turn it off.

I wish this song were done, pa-rum-pum-pum-pum
Go get my gun . . .

"So what do you want for Christmas?" she had asked him two days ago, having forgotten what he'd said about the Pacific.

"Hawaii," he said. "All I want for Christmas is warmth and sunshine. I am desperate for sunlight. The freedom of walking out the door in your shorts and T-shirt and into a warm and welcoming atmosphere. You feel the same way. Admit it. So let's go. Christmas is meant to be pleasurable. A time when we rise above petty materialism and do our best to make each other happy."

"Oh darling, I'm tired of having this conversation, so let's not. You can have a perfectly lovely Christmas right here in Minneapolis if you put your mind to it."

Joyce was careful about money, having grown up frugal in Wauwatosa, with parents who saved plastic bags, glass jars, and jar lids, thousands of lids, perfectly clean, stored in plastic bags, a drawer full of used tinfoil carefully washed. Plus she was afflicted with liberal guilt: about the fuel consumption of jet airliners and the effect of the exhaust on the ozone layer and about the *idea* of vacations—should they not be taking disadvantaged children with them, underprivileged children with learning disabilities?

He did not care to have disadvantaged children with him in Hawaii. He had been disadvantaged at one time himself and now, as a recovering disadvantaged child, he had learned to enjoy pleasure, actually enjoy it, not merely tolerate it, but Mrs. Sparrow remembered their last vacation—to Mackinac Island, where they were waited on by old black men in starched white uniforms and she fretted about that and the fresh-cut flowers on the tables and how much they were paying for this Pinot Noir with elegant structure and an extended palate, complex and bright on a tannic frame, nicely oaked with a lingering finish of boysenberries, sheepskin, and pencil shavings, and what that money could do if you donated it to a relief organization for digging wells for African villages where people perished for want of clean water.

He clicked a switch on the radio and a different song came on:

Woke up this morning like my heart would break
Blues in my coffee, blues in my fruitcake,

But I want to go down to the shopping mall
And let the longest train I ever saw come and pacify my
  mind
'Cause I got shackles on my feet and the water tastes like
  turpentine
And I'm rolling from side to side and can't keep from
  cryin'
Because my baby she treats me so unkind.

It was the Moondog show on AM77, which sometimes, in bouts of insomnia, he tuned in to for a fitful hour or two to hear the Moondog talk about Fanny May and how she tormented him with her loving words and then without warning she told him to go away and he wound up in Joey's Bar and Grill looking down into the whiskey in his glass and got good and drunk and went contrite and weeping to Fanny May's house and knocked on her door and she would not let him in. Other talk show hosts railed about pointy-headed liberals, but that was much less interesting than a beautiful woman who drives you crazy because you can't live without her.

"We were fixing to go to Fanny May's family's for Christmas and then she accused me of not caring about her family, which isn't true, it just isn't true. It's just that her family talks *all the time*, and I can't get a word in edgewise, but she says I am *sullen* around her family. That's crazy!" said Moondog, strumming his old Gibson guitar named Mona. "So yesterday I spent all afternoon shopping for a Christmas gift for Fanny May, trying to make up with her. I looked at velveteen cocktail dresses and silk blouses and jewelry, and I'm thinking, 'Anything I like, she won't. My darling love and I do not agree in matters of taste. Guaranteed. I love sweet and she prefers sour. I choose white and she wants black. So why do I bother?' People, listen to me. I looked at a miniature Swiss village made of porcelain with clock tower and church steeple and people sliding down a hill on tiny toboggans and couples skating on a pond. Beautiful. I knew she'd think it was trashy. Looked at big picture books. Cézanne. Montana. *Anne of Green Gables.* Clark Gable. Lewis and Clark. Looked at digital cameras, telescopes on tripods, white Turkish bathrobes, cosmetics, a perfume that cost *one hundred dollars an ounce.* And everything I looked at, I could hear Fanny May say, *You really thought I'd like* that?"

Moondog was on a rant, and then—*click*. The radio switched over, of its own free will, to a choir calling for the faithful to come joyful and triumphant to Bethlehem, which brought back a painful memory of the high school Christmas choral recital in Looseleaf, North Dakota—standing in the baritone section in his blue robe, needing badly to pee, humming "Adeste Fideles" and processing out of the candle-lit gymnasium, his bladder aching, marching under the watchful gaze of the town and down the stairs to the choir room and hurrying out of the robe and stepping on the hem and ripping it and dashing off to the toilet. Christmas was a sad time for the Sparrows. Their tree was a scrawny thing, and Mother lived in fear that it would burst into flames and they would die in their sleep of smoke inhalation. Daddy lived in fear that Mother would spend them into bankruptcy and they would have to go live in a public institution and wear orange jumpsuits and pick up trash along the highway.

O come all ye faithful,
Fearful and deluded,
Come ye, O come ye, to North Dakota.

"Darling?" he said. "Darling?" She opened her eyes, the comforter pulled up to her chin, her dark hair splayed against the pillow. She pulled an earplug out.

"How do you get rid of this stupid music?" She looked up at him in wonderment. So he repeated the question.

"The radio is voice controlled," she said. "You just say *OFF.*" And the music stopped.

2. Unpleasant memories
of the joyous season

"What time is it?" she said.

"Almost six o'clock."

"Why?"

"It just is. I'm sorry I woke you. Go back to sleep."

"I can't." She sat up. "God, I am so sick. Some horrible flu virus. I should have stayed home from work yesterday. This bozo came in and stood over my desk and he was sneezing all over me. No hanky, nothing—just leaned back and barked and let fly with thousands of tiny beads of infection flying in the air."

"You'd feel better if we went to a warm place."

"Oh darling, I can't bear the thought of getting on a plane. I am sick to my stomach."

And with that she threw off the covers and leaped toward the bathroom in three bounds and slammed the door and he heard water running in the sink and other more visceral sounds and he was transported back to the terrible Christmas when the Dark Angel of Projectile Vomiting visited the Sparrows of Looseleaf. Oh my gosh, what a vivid memory it was. Twenty-five years ago and still he could feel the gorge rising in the pit of his stomach, the acid bubbling up, the sphincter straining. He was seventeen and that day in school he had suffered the most harrowing humiliation of his life, standing in front of twenty leering choir members as Miss Forsberg cried, "Tenors, open your mouths. You can't sing with your mouths shut. Basses, read the notes. They're right in front of you." And she nodded to him, and he started to sing, "Why do the nations so furiously rage together," and what came out was *Wfmrghghghgh* and the sopranos chortled like hyenas, and Miss Forsberg said, "Again!" and he screwed it up again. Choked. He slunk home from choir, running the gauntlet of snowballers—and in Looseleaf, the snowballs were hard and thrown sidearm with deadly accuracy—and he found Mother making the stuffing to put in the turkey and she was weeping over their imminent deaths, which she could see only too clearly:

FAMILY OF FIVE DIES IN CHRISTMAS EVE FIRE;
FAULTY WIRING FINGERED AS CAUSE;
CHRISTMAS TREE LIGHTS EXPLODED AROUND 2 A.M.;
RESCUERS UNABLE TO FIGHT WAY THROUGH FLAMES;

**PITIFUL SHRIEKS HEARD FROM UPSTAIRS BEDROOM;
NEIGHBORS PLACE MEMORIAL WREATHS AT SITE;
"A NICE FAMILY," SAYS ONE, "KEPT TO THEMSELVES
BUT ALWAYS FRIENDLY AND WILLING TO HELP."**

The moment Mother turned on the lights on the tree, she could smell smoke and hear sirens in her mind, hear the shouts of firemen. (*Up here. On the roof!*) So she checked the Christmas tree frequently for signs of combustion, and he tried to tell her that choir was twisting him into knots and he wanted to quit choir forever, otherwise he would go berserk and probably commit an act of senseless violence, but she stood there pouring freshwater into the tree stand and pruning the dry branches, not listening. Meanwhile, Daddy was ranting and raving about money. "I will never understand to the end of my born days," he said, "how someone can leave a room without turning off the lights. How much exertion does it take to reach up and snap off a light switch? You must think we are Hollywood stars made of money to see this house with lights blazing at night."

Mother heard the word "blazing" and shuddered at the thought. A Christmas tree blazing up and burning down your house. The irony of it: you bring a thing of beauty and magic into your home, and it turns around and kills you. The lights left on too long, the tree not properly watered, the family exhausted from the festivities, and in the wee hours—*poof!* Spontaneous combustion! A deadly conflagration. The family vaporized. Small blackened corpses in little white coffins, weeping relatives carrying them into the cemetery. She felt weak in the knees and had to sit down. And then felt sick to her stomach.

Daddy looked at the stack of presents under the tree and cried out, "You've gone mad! You must think I am made of money! What possessed you, woman? I am only a municipal employee. I am not John D. Rockefeller!"

That was the year she gave Daddy a pair of bedroom slippers with lights in the toes. He looked at her with narrowed eyes. "You've got to bend down to turn them off and on," he said. "This is the dumbest damn thing I ever saw." She said, "Well, you need to get up in the night a lot, so I thought these would help you see your way to the bathroom." He said, "You ever hear of the flashlight? It's a great invention. We've got five of them around the house. I think I'm all set."

Mother went off to the bedroom to cry, and Daddy looked at him and said, "Well, James, that's Christmas for you. You don't want it, you don't need it, and you'll pay for it the rest of the year."

And that was the year she gave James a used book for Christmas. Also a Boy Scout telescope and a transistor radio and a pair of corduroys, but the main item was a copy of *Foxx's Book of Christian Martyrs* inscribed faintly in pencil, "To Esther, from your brother Elwyn, Christmas 1951." He showed it to Mother and she said, "Oh, well, you can erase that." She said, "It was the only copy they had, and I thought you might enjoy it. I did, when I was your age." He read a few pages, all about French Protestants being burned at the stake, or crushed under rocks, or crucified, or drowned, or torn apart by teams of horses hitched to their arms, or whipped to ribbons. One horror after another.

And then the projectile vomiting got under way. His little sister, Elaine, and brother, Benny, lay in their beds upstairs, the smell of Lysol in the air, and moaned and complained of fever and nausea, a basin on the floor into which they yorked up their RyKrisp and ginger ale. James was sent up to empty the basin in the toilet and rinse it out.

"Is Santa here?" cried the little tykes.

"You expect Santa to come and breathe your germs and spread them to every other boy and girl on this planet so that there is a mass epidemic of puking and pooping all over the world? What sort of Christmas would that be? Millions of children waking up on Christmas morning in a pool of green poop? Of course Santa isn't going to come. Forget about it." They put their hot little faces into their pillows and sobbed heart-wrenching sobs, and he went downstairs and soon began to feel queasy himself.

And just then, as he heard Mother pour buttermilk into a bowl to make custard, the Dark Angel touched his shoulder and he had to dash to the bathroom—and the door was locked. He knocked four loud knocks. Daddy said, "Go away! Occupied!" So he dashed outdoors and there, in a snowdrift near the back door, it exploded out of him at both ends. Stomach and bowels. Chunks of many colors. He scooped up snow to hide his disgrace, but it soaked right in. He took off his pants and stuffed them into the garbage can, and turned and saw Mrs. Tippett's face at the kitchen window staring at him, and then she ducked away. She had seen. His shame was public. Soon the word would flash around Looseleaf that Jimmy Sparrow had shit his pants. He hid behind the garage and washed himself with snow, and snuck into the house full of Christmas lights and a radio choir and slunk up to his bed and spent a whole day of invalidism lying very quietly, not eating anything or thinking about eating or wanting to hear about anybody eating, feeling like the object of a cruel experiment.

Christmas was the emotional high-water mark of Lutheran life in Looseleaf, which, like the highest elevation in North Dakota, is not exactly *high*—not *high high*, but still, there was a sense of beauty and overwhelming feeling, and when the choir sang, "Jeg Er Så Glad Hver Julekveld," about Jesus born under the bright stars as the angels sang so sweetly, people wept, people who you thought were incapable of tears, their eyes filled up and tears ran down their stone cheeks, a miracle. And so, when you wound up sick and stinky out in the snow with the neighbors looking out their windows at you, it was a long fall from a great height. Still painful after all these years.

Mrs. Sparrow was very quiet in the bathroom. He knocked on the door. "Are you all right?" There was a groan from inside. "Would you care for a ginger ale? Some toast and tea?"

"No," she said. She opened the door. She had washed her face and she looked up at him all beautiful and needy and he put his arms around her. "There's no need to suffer," he said. "How about I call a doctor?"

"No need to waste a doctor's time. It's the common flu, darling, or whatever that jerk was passing around. I guess I'll just stay in bed for Christmas."

He was going to say something about Hawaii and then didn't. He put on his black bathrobe and walked barefoot across the wood floor. A mirror hung on the wall and he ducked it. Didn't want to see his face just now. His bland face with the light green, almost yellowish eyes—"gecko eyes" Cousin Liz called them when they were kids. In the kitchen, overlooking Lake Calhoun, he poured water in the coffee-maker and filled the basket with ground coffee and his eye caught the woman in the white bathrobe walking through the snow on the wooden deck behind the big white house on the lake shore. Steam rose from a big hot tub, and she pulled off the cover and more steam boiled up into the cold night air. She stripped off her bathrobe and climbed in, one grace-ful motion, her pale nakedness visible for one brief moment, and then sat, water up to her chin, snow falling on her blond head, the darkness of the lake beyond. He had seen her at St. Ansgar's. A divorced woman, no kids, living on the for-tune her lawyers had wrested from her car-dealer husband, who, after the divorce, had spiraled down and down through two girlfriends, several lawsuits, bankruptcy, and into a ten-year prison stay for mail fraud. He had grown tired of this pale, radiant goddess and left her for a life of shame and anguish. A good object lesson, this naked beauty in the snow. He wished she would climb out and perhaps comb her hair, but she did not.

Her beauty reminded him of Kuhikuhikapapa'u'mau-mau—the tranquility of the place in the evenings when they walked down the great lawn to the white beach and dropped their robes and plunged naked into the sea and swam out a hundred yards and floated there as the sun went down, to see the lights come on in the main lodge with the lanai and the portico around the pool, an ivory palace under the sheltering palms, as they floated in the arms of the ever-lasting sea, inhaling the salt air and the sweet, blossomy breeze, listening to the pianist play a Chopin etude, and the two of them transcended the Midwest and entered into a state of buoyant blessedness.

He poured a cup of coffee and looked down at the blond

head and the pale shoulders in the steaming tub and wished he had that kind of money, to own a mansion overlooking the lake. Or that he knew someone who did. Such as Mrs. Blondie, for example. Mr. Sparrow was a faithful husband, but that didn't preclude a little daydreaming. He could imagine nestling in the hot tub next to the pale radiance, and her saying, "When do we fly to Hawaii?" and him saying, "Whenever you like. The jet is waiting, I'll call the pilots whenever you like."

3. A brief digression on coyotes

Mr. Morosco was not sleeping well these days and was sending out e-mails at three and four in the morning, which he expected you to deal with ASAP, which meant 6:00 or 7:00 a.m., and if he didn't get a reply by 8:00, he could be imperious. Mr. Sparrow checked his e-mail and found one from 2:34 a.m. "Where in blazes is my memoir?" Mr. Morosco had written. "You were supposed to have that to me this week."

Running with Coyotes, by Billy J. Morosco, was Mr. Sparrow's current project, and it was taking longer than expected because the story kept changing. Mr. Morosco had always said that he bought the company's energy drink formula for $250 from an old chemist in the Wrangler Saloon in Livingston, Montana, back when he was thirty-two, a salesman for a peanut brittle company, with no bright prospects in life, driving around the Great Plains, staying at budget motels, making the rounds. But he'd told Mr. Sparrow that he won the formula in a poker game, one night in Livingston, drawing a royal flush and taking a piece of paper with numbers and letters on it, which he had a laboratory work up and produce Coyote juice.

Now Mr. Sparrow was told that Mr. Morosco had been driving around Montana with a ski mask and a Colt pistol sticking up convenience stores. This word came from a disgruntled cousin, Emmett Frayne of Missoula, who claimed to have hidden Mr. Morosco when the FBI was on his tail.

"I was in Livingston with B.J. when he pulled his one and only bank job. I drove the car. We were sitting in the parking lot and he had the ski mask on top of his head and he was composing the stickup note when these two men galloped toward the bank wearing Donald Duck masks, pistols in hand. Their eye holes must've been not lined up right because they ran right into a sculpture of a boy and his dog—one hit the boy, the other the dog—and whacked themselves in the gonads and fell to the ground, where a female security guard sprayed them in the snoot with pepper spray and they were dragged off to the pokey. B.J. turned to me and said, 'I am giving up robbery.' And he threw his mask in the trash and ripped up the note and we went to the bar to celebrate and, yes, there was an old chemist there and he was roaring drunk, but there was no game of poker. He asked B.J. for a loan, and B.J. gave him ten bucks, and the old guy handed over the formula and said, 'This is great stuff to put the lead in your pencil,' but he didn't tell B.J. he could go ahead and manufacture the stuff. The old chemist had been fired after thirty-two years at Monsanto. He was a drunk. But he still has his rights and he didn't sign them over to B.J. Not while I was there."

Mr. Morosco had always said that he gave the chemist extra money to get to Phoenix to see his sister. Emmett disagreed. "Hogwash," he said. "Never gave him a cent."

Mr. Morosco said he took the formula to a lab in Chicago. Minneapolis, said Emmett. They came up with a compound that seemed to get a person all wired up, and he marketed it through the Internet back when the Net was like a secret society, and within a year he had a factory in Antigua going full steam and a mail room with fifty employees shipping the packages out by the truckload. Oddly, Coyote had little or no effect on Mr. Morosco. It only made him irritable.

Emmett was on the phone with Mr. Sparrow for more than an hour for that interview, and then mailed him a photograph of Mr. Morosco as a wiry guy with curly black hair, lining up a pool shot, a cigarette on his lower lip and smoke in his face, wearing tight jeans and a Western shirt, looking like Woody Guthrie. Now he was cruising at a comfortable altitude in life, about fifty pounds heavier, hair thinner, and Mr. Sparrow was okay with writing Mr. Morosco's version

of his own life, including his preachments on the value of
hard work and taking chances on behalf of your dream, et
cetera, but Mr. Sparrow was uneasy about including Mr.
Morosco's thoughts about coyotes.

Americans have become soft, a nation of couch potatoes, and we're losing ground to the coyotes, who are
moving in on us, taking over large sections of the
country. Even in Manhattan. Coyotes travel into
the city through tunnels and they rule Central Park
at night. Many children whose pictures are on milk
cartons were taken by coyotes and raised by coyotes,
living in caves, learning to move swiftly undetected
and to gather food and to stay with the pack. Americans sit in their overheated or overcooled houses,
ensnared in the narcissism of Facebook and the nar-
cotic of TV, and outside, glittering eyes are watching
them. Coyote trails wind through the backyards and
close to schools, where mysterious children arrive in
the morning, wearing old clothes, smelling of earth,
their hair wild and their teeth yellow, but they are
completely focused, their gaze an unrelenting gaze,
watching, learning, waiting.

I believe that I lived with coyotes one summer
when I was thirteen, a repressed memory that was
regained through hypnosis, and I believe I learned the

things that enable me to run a corporation that grosses $40 million a year and is growing steadily.

Mr. Morosco insisted that his coyote philosophy go into the book, including his extensive recollection of life in the pack when he was thirteen. He had called Mr. Sparrow into his office and spoken at great length about that summer and had demonstrated the coyote language of snuffling and chuffing, and he had crawled on all fours over to a potted plant and lifted his right leg and peed on it. The man was insane. Mr. Sparrow was fairly sure that when the memoir was published, if the coyote part was discovered by the press, it would be front-page news and the company's stock would go in the toilet and that he, James Sparrow, would be blamed for it. He wanted to bury the coyote stuff in a long appendix ("My Credo") among long quotes from Hermann Hesse and Thoreau, but Mr. Morosco insisted on starting the book with his memory of living with coyotes.

His e-mail read:

Jim, very important to put Life w. Coyotes front & center. This is a recovered memory from my 6 mos. of therapy w. Ginger. Most fantastic experience of my life. Highly recommended. What a woman. She pulled things out of me I never knew were there.

So when do I get to see the book?

Mr. Sparrow fired back an e-mail: "It's a beautiful memoir and it will be ready in its own good time. I want it to be of excellent quality, and so do you. Merry Christmas."

And he thought that now would be the perfect time to retreat to Kuhikuhikapapa'u'maumau and lie in a hammock under the fragrant frangipani trees above the white beach, eating fresh sliced mango. A little R & R before the fertilizer hit the ventilator.

4. A rocky beginning to a difficult day

The pale, radiant, naked woman put her white bath-robe back on and disappeared into her mansion, and Mr. Sparrow watched the headlights of cars wind along Lake Street toward downtown, heading for the salt mines. The red flasher of a chopper went whumping over-head. Minneapolis lay under a pile of dark clouds and he could feel the cold steel gates of winter closing down.

And now an e-mail from Simon in the Coyote PR depart-ment. The Minneapolis *Star-Tribune* was inquiring as to Mr. Morosco's net worth—was it $130 million? Was it more? They wanted to know because a Salvation Army Santa Claus had filed a lawsuit alleging that Mr. Morosco had punched him when he asked Mr. Morosco to put additional money into the bucket as Mr. Morosco emerged from Macy's with an armload of gifts. The Santa, bruised and disheartened, had retreated to a nearby cocktail lounge and tied one on and had to be shoveled into rehab. The *Star-Tribune* wanted a comment. He called Simon at home.

"What to do?" said Simon.

"No comment on that," he replied. "None. Just say that Mr. Morosco gives the Salvation Army thousands every year."

"Does he?"

"He will now."

He could hear Mrs. Sparrow return in great haste to the bathroom, retching, spitting. He opened the front door and picked up the *Star-Tribune* off the doormat. Nothing about Mr. Morosco on the front page. The top headline was:

BLIZZARD DEATH TOLL STANDS AT TWO

A Butte, Montana, man died yesterday after he and his wife, 67, left home in their shirtsleeves to drive to the airport to fly to Tampa, not knowing the parking ramp was full and they would have to park in the overflow lot. The man, who also was 67, dropped his wife off at the terminal and parked the car and waited for the shuttle bus, which never came due to scheduling problems. "Had Bernie walked briskly to the terminal and not waited around, he would still be alive today," said Sgt. Matt Hazzard of the airport police, who announced the victim's name as Bernie Rose. "We had thirteen wonderful years together and then God took him home," said Mrs. Rose from Tampa, where she flew as scheduled. "Bernie was a man who embraced life, and that's what I'm doing." Services will be held in the spring, she said, when the ground warms up.

Meanwhile, in Casper, Wyoming, a rancher suffering from cabin fever tried to thaw out his car with a shovelful of red-hot coals, and the car caught fire. So he got out a toboggan and hitched up two steers to it and they pulled him for 4.2 miles down the road at high speed and then the two divided to go around a telephone pole, where the man died of the impact. He was 47. His name was Carl Koehler. Neighbors said he was quiet and kept to himself.

In Tarpon Springs, Florida, a missing St. Paul man named Buehler was located in an enormous nursing facility. He had retired from the police force and moved to Florida with his wife, Lurleen, and the climate change threw his immune system out of whack. He caught a virus that wouldn't go away, wound up in a hospital inside a plastic bubble with tubes running in and out, and dementia set in, and meanwhile she had fallen in love with a surf instructor named Speedy and didn't visit Mr. Buehler for several weeks while she took up surfing. He disappeared from the hospital. He was found three months later in a nursing facility police described as a "warehouse for transplant harvests," comatose people on life support in hygienic containers, all of them Midwesterners, big, sturdy people, farmers, cops, truck drivers, brought down by climate-related illness, kept alive as their organs were harvested—eyeballs, bone marrow, a kidney, skin, whatever was needed—and sold on the black market. A detective said, "You walk around among the super-rich in Naples and look into people's eyes and there are Midwestern eyes, the corneas of old farmers. It's a billion-dollar-a-year business and we don't know how to stop it."

A downer of an article, one more reason not to read a newspaper. But it stuck with him. Go to a warmer climate and wind up as an organ donor.

"Darling?" He heard footsteps in the hall. Mrs. Sparrow came around the corner looking like a poor wretch straight out of Dickens, sweaty, pale, trembly, and sat down at the table. He put his arm around her, and she nestled into his side. "Please don't leave me," she said.

"Never," he said.

"Promise."

"I promise."

5. He wishes only for a little pleasure—is that too much to ask?

Mrs. Sparrow had no appetite for breakfast. She had lost last night's dinner and taken a glass of Everwell Crystals to quell the uprising, and now she needed to get her mind off her digestive tract. She thought she would feel better if she took a brisk walk to the Art Institute and looked around in the French Impressionists section and visited the Renoir painting of the chef in white, which reminded her of Al's Breakfast Nook in Minneapolis, where she enjoyed a cheesy meatloaf omelet every morning during her unhappy year going for her MFA in theater. All she learned, despite the effusive praise of her instructors, was that she was a lousy actor. She was smart and attractive and could speak brightly and clearly, but she had nothing whatsoever to give an audience. She was flat, dry, dim, empty. The fry cook in Al's put more heart into an omelet than she had onstage. She sat in the diner, nursing a cup of bitter coffee and wishing she could experience some personal tragedy, an addiction perhaps, the loss of a parent, a mysterious disease, some grief she could draw upon to deepen her acting, but she was basically a happy, well-organized person in good health. She sat in Al's and wept about this. And the fry cook asked if she was all right, and she smiled up at him and said, "Never better." Which, unfortunately, was true.

Mrs. Sparrow cried often and cried beautifully, and her husband had learned in eleven years of marriage that crying was part of her makeup and didn't indicate unhappiness, and that the worst thing he could say was "What's wrong?" Nothing. She was clearing out her system, as simple as exhaling.

She cried looking at certain paintings, and hearing *Madama Butterfly*, and at Mimì's death in *La Bohème*, and at movies when the heroine was diagnosed with a deadly disease or the boy was ridiculed by his drunken father or the lovers bade each other a chill farewell, and she wept at *A Christmas Carol* when Scrooge was guided by the Ghost to see that his love of the bountiful Belle had been destroyed by his sour passion for earning money. She loved those redemptive stories in which some cruel, hard-hearted skeptic hates Christmas and then sees a bright star in the sky, or a candle in a window, or a child's face lit up in wonder, and his heart melts and he falls to his knees and repents.

"I wish you'd come see *A Christmas Carol* with me," she

said. "The ghosts are wonderful this year. And Scrooge is electric."

"I saw the movie when I was a kid and found it terrifying. No need to repeat the experience."

She smiled at him sweetly. "I wish you enjoyed Christmas. Somehow I feel it's my fault. I haven't given you the Christmas you deserve."

"I might like Christmas more if it were in June," he said. "There's no good reason for it to be on December twenty-fifth. There is no snow and ice in the Christmas story. The shepherds were out in the fields, for God's sake. Only reason they put it in December was to take over the old pagan holiday of Saturnalia and Christianize it, sort of like you'd buy up a theater and turn it into a church."

"It's the spirit of it that hits you so hard, darling. You're sentimental and you have to guard against it and that's why you put up that hard exterior. It's the sure sign of a soft heart."

Nice of her to think so, but not true. Not true. Christmas brought back powerful, painful memories of winter in Looseleaf, North Dakota. The little white house and the wind blowing and the ice on the windows and the terrible cold in the house. The African violets died and the cactus; some ferns survived and a rubber plant; but there was a funereal air about winter. Daddy believed that if you couldn't see your breath when you talked, then the furnace

37

was turned up too high, not that their family talked—they did not need to talk—they knew one another only too well without conversing, but they did respirate as they sat around the kitchen table under the Praying Hands plaque and ate their wieners and fried potatoes and clouds of steam came out of their mouths. Winter was like a prison camp. Any sort of playfulness or jokiness was discouraged. No reading at the table. Daddy said things like "I don't know how I am going to make it through this week." And the statement sat there, a general lament at the state of things, and nobody said a word. The tyranny of complaint. It trumps everything else.

After supper Daddy listened to *Friendly Neighbors* on WLT as Mother washed the dishes and James curled up with his *World Almanac*, which he'd read so many times he knew the major exports of all nations by heart, the state capitals and every member of the U.S. Senate, and the top batters in the American and National leagues, but it was a ten-year-old almanac—Daddy refused to buy a new one—and some of the batters had retired. Bedtime was 9:00 p.m. (What else was there to do?) Mother and Daddy slept in the downstairs bedroom in a sagging double bed, and James and Elaine and Benny slept in the cold attic on narrow, hard beds. Heat was supposed to rise, but it didn't in this house. They wore woolen long underwear to bed and heavy socks, and there was no thought of bedwetting—it simply wasn't an option.

They slept in the cold sheets and awoke with full bladders and pulled on layers of clothing and ran downstairs to the toilet and ate breakfast and put on more clothing. It was in the time before lightweight thermal wear; you kept warm by the exertion of carrying heavy clothing. You ate your Hot Ralston and put on the parka and the four-buckle overshoes and out the door you went, into the world of blazing white blizzard, and you trudged a quarter mile to the road where the boys had made a snow fort and the girls huddled together, and the boys peed in the snow as a defense against wolves, and the girls crouched, shivering, whimpering, waiting for the bus to come. A long wait. Your toes got numb and you started to imagine frostbite and gangrene and amputation and a life without feet. And then someone whooped, and the bus appeared, a blot of yellow in the storm.

Memories of grim winter mornings came back to him every December, and he felt a skittery panic at the first snowfall, and as Christmas approached, he felt a sort of quiet terror. It was the Tongue on the Pump Handle Syndrome.

His mother used to warn him about frostbite—*wear warm socks and mittens*—and she warned him to always breathe through his nose, not his mouth, so the air would be warmed before it reached the lungs—"You don't want to frost your lungs," she said—and she warned against putting your tongue on a pump handle. Your tongue would freeze to it, and there you'd be, stuck, and somebody would have to come

39

and rip your tongue off it, causing horrible pain, and you would talk with a lisp afterward, even after years of speech therapy, and people would talk about it behind your back. ("He put his tongue on a pump handle. Deranged. Gone in the head. Nice family, but he's crazier than a hoot owl.")

The tongue-on-the-pump-handle dilemma loomed large in his mind for some reason, though pump handles were a rarity. He mentioned this to his sister, Elaine, who said, "Mother always was worried about you because you were sickly and difficult and didn't get along with other children. Eventually they had programs for special-needs kids like you, but they didn't then. There was only your mom."

"Special needs? Me?"

"Look at you. You're all screwed up. You can't bear Christmas."

"And that makes me a special-needs person?"

"I read an article about OCYD. Obsessive-Compulsive Yule Dread. It's a form of paranoia. Pump handles are a symbol of you-know-what."

"What?"

"You know."

"I don't think so."

"You don't know."

It wasn't only pump handles—it was also poles, pillars, pipes, pegs, pins, pommels, pendulums, propellers, spindles, sprockets, and spacers—but he didn't confess that to Elaine.

He went to a psychiatrist named Walters, who dashed off a prescription for something called Mist on the Mountains and told him to take two right away and then one a day in the morning with food (but not with celery).

"What is this?" he asked the psychiatrist.

"Antidepressant."

"Is it going to help?"

"If it doesn't, we'll try something else."

"What does it do?"

"What do you mean, 'What does it do?' It's an antidepressant. It makes you happy. It induces amnesia and it snip-snip-snips the thread of memory, and all those bad memories go drifting away like dirty bathwater and you'll be boyish and ebullient again."

"Will I still be able to read and write?"

"Probably."

"*Probably!?*"

"There are trade-offs," said the psychiatrist. "But listen—you don't want it? Fine. I'll save it for somebody else. And good luck." And presented a bill for $220 for consultation.

Pump-Handle Syndrome. He Googled it and found an article by psychophysiologist Dr. Heinrich Hertz, an expert on polar obsessions, a professor in the *Zentral Kontor zie Ordnung Zusammenschluss Medizinisch Forschung Verbindung Geschloss*. In the article (entitled "*Gespruchen*

zie daskompenforshnittgennocktvairbruggendeehompen")
Hertz recommended that syndrome sufferers move to a
warmer climate.

If only.

At Elaine's urging, he went to a psychologist, Dr. Boemer,
who told him that he exhibited symptoms of obsessive-
compulsive behavior, and Dr. Boemer got to talking about
other OCD cases he'd seen—obsessive hand-wringing, obsessive counting of ceiling tiles, obsessive ironing and pacing
and talking, obsessive Facebook updating and friending, a
male patient who went to a gym three times a day to shoot
free throws, exactly three hundred each time, and how Dr.
Boemer had gotten him down to one hundred. Dr. Boemer
was fascinated by OCD and he told about case after case.
Obsessive-compulsive piano practicing. Guitar tuning. Making of lists. Clipping articles from newspapers and filing
them. Nose picking. E-mailing jokes. One of his patients ob-
sessively brushed her teeth down to tiny stumps. Another
made bomb threats, hundreds a day, but always honking an
ooga-ooga horn, so they'd know it wasn't for real.

Dr. Boemer went on and on as Mr. Sparrow stood with his
hand on the doorknob and Dr. Boemer could not stop telling
him about obsessive treadmill running, obsessive copyedit-
ing and grammar correcting, solitaire playing, throat clearing, belly itching, Web surfing, folk dancing, photography,
pants adjusting, geyser gazing, apologizing. He had a client

named Mrs. Sanderson who could not speak a simple sentence without prefacing it with a "So anyway." Mr. Sparrow said, "Excuse me but I'm fairly certain that it's a violation of medical ethics to disclose these details," and Dr. Boemer said, "There was this one guy I recall who hummed to himself. Boy, that was a case. We worked on him for almost two years."

Mr. Sparrow left and never went back. His tongue-on-the-pump-handle fear remained strong. The only solution was Kuhikuhikapapa'u'maumau. He imagined a pop-up on his computer screen: *Guess what? You've just won forty thousand dollars!* Or a canvas bag falling off a speeding Brink's truck. A kindly gentleman stepping out of a black limo: "I noticed that you helped that old blind lady find her doctor's office," he would murmur. "I'm sure it wasn't the first time you've taken time to help others. Please accept this gift from the Samaritan Foundation." A check for a hundred grand. They could buy their way out of this miserable condo with its thin walls and bad plumbing, and they could find a place in the paradise of Hawaii.

6. Mrs. Manicotti

He stood under the hot shower spray and, without thinking, pressed his tongue against the hot-water pipe and recoiled and slipped slightly, and sharp pain shot up his lower back. He toweled off and put on his black jockeys, a pair of chinos, and a white shirt and lay in the hallway and did his back-stretching exercises and was in the middle of the rump raise when the phone rang. He let it go to voice mail and heard the voice of his cousin Liz in Looseleaf. "Call me when you have a minute," she said.

Well, he had plenty of minutes but he wasn't keen on listening to Liz talk about the ruinous state of the country, the national debt, what liberals have done to our schools, the spinelessness of politicians, the tyranny of unions, the unconstitutionality of gun control and taxation, the cowardice of our foreign policy, so he put off calling her and switched on the TV and got engrossed in a documentary about penguins. Lines of the fellows marching like black robots across the ice and popping into the water. And then one penguin in the jaws of a sea lion, hauled away for dinner flailing and squeaking. Which made Mr. Sparrow think of the Coyote Corp. and the security men who likely would meet him at the headquarters door on Monday morning. His badge and keys would be confiscated. He'd be ordered to pack up his personal things in a cardboard box while security observed, and then he'd be escorted out to his car in the parking lot. His parking permit would be torn from the visor. "Good-bye and good luck," the security guy would say, and Mr. Sparrow would drive out of the lot and—do what? Go to a bar and order a bloody Mary? Come home and watch TV? What do you do when you've been de-pantsed? He'd look for a new job, probably, and find one as a parking lot attendant downtown. Wear a blue work shirt with "Zippy Park" embroidered on the pocket and sit in a little shack, and when the big shots wheeled in and hopped out, you said, "Thank you, sir," and parked their cars, bowing slightly, and if some old colleague from Coyote drove in, you'd chat with him for a minute, neither of you remarking on the obvious—your fall into disgrace—and then you'd park his lovely BMW and try not to brood about the injustice of it all. That goofball idiot was kept on the payroll while loyal hardworking you got the shaft.

Joyce returned from her walk at 10:44 a.m. and said it was brisk and bracing outdoors and good for her ailment. She took off her wire-rim glasses and stood across the table, this tall broad-shouldered woman with mahogany hair tied back in a copper clip, grinning at him, crinkling her Roman nose, in her cowboy shirt and gray sweatpants, the sheer elegance of her, and he stood up and put his arms around her, tears in his eyes.

He'd met her the same year he joined Coyote Corp. and accompanied Billy Jack, who was judging a Christmas Gift-Wrap Contest at Marshall Field, which she won in the final round, the globular round, wrapping a basketball in golden paper, and hers had not a wrinkle or crinkle or rip in it. And he sat next to her at the awards luncheon and she talked about her aspirations in theater and he listened and he proposed a weekend at Mackinac Island and she told him that she would feel terrible guilt about such a thing because during her acting-school days in New York she had, in order to protect her cheap sublet of an apartment on West Seventy-first and Broadway, dressed up in a black silk dress and a mantilla and attended early morning Mass, impersonating the old lady from whom she'd sublet and who had died, thus rendering the sublet invalid, and after eight months in the role of Mrs. Manicotti she came to feel a true religious devotion she had not felt as a Methodist in Wauwatosa, which caused a rift with her family, who were willing to accept agnosticism, but Catholicism was another matter.

"Whatever we are—and it does vary from week to week—we are not Catholic," said her mother. "We do not kneel at statues. We do not inhale incense or ding little bells.

We do not kiss the ring of some old Italian guy in a white dress. We do not treat women as brood sows." But Joyce loved the kneeling part, especially at midnight Mass at the Church of the Holy Sacrament on Christmas Eve, when her faith was miraculously renewed. She felt the Holy Child's dear presence, His gentle touch, His sweet breath, and when the assemblage knelt—the mixed assortment you find in a New York church, various oddballs and lunatics, old character actors, old black ladies, gay couples, Puerto Rican cleaning ladies, the elderly up front and the punky young to the rear—and quietly sang "Silent Night," she felt transformed, and every Christmas thereafter she relived that night in New York and the holy hush that descended on her life. So she could not traipse off to Mackinac Island with him.

She told him the whole long story in the restaurant and then in his apartment on a couch in front of a gas fireplace, and he told her he respected her feelings, though he wanted terribly to make love, and she fell asleep with her head on his lap, and they dated chastely for all of four months until her Mrs. Manicotti persona permitted greater intimacy, and after that came eleven years of pleasant marriage, except for the Christmas holidays, of which this one was shaping up (he thought) to be the worst.

She had dressed and gone out for a walk while he watched the penguins, and she returned feeling better. So he mentioned Hawaii. "I just figured out that, using frequent-flier mileage and getting the cheapest room in the main lodge, we could get a week at Kuhikuhikapapa'u'maumau for under a thousand dollars for the two of us."

"I thought we wanted to invite your sister, Elaine—she's all alone."

"Elaine is a mess. Let's not spend the holiday doing intervention therapy."

"I loved Kuhikuhikapapa'u'maumau. It's beautiful. It just seems like an odd way to spend Christmas. At a beach, wearing a bikini."

"I'll buy you a Christmas bikini."

"Oh darling—I want to have a Christmas tree."

"They'll have that at the resort."

"I want my own."

He thought, *Maybe I need to tell her about the pump-handle problem, how it's come back to haunt me.*

She said, "I have all these plans, darling. I have tickets for *Hansel and Gretel* at the opera and *A Child's Christmas in Wales* and the *Bach Christmas Oratorio,* and I can't possibly go to Hawaii for Christmas."

She said, "I'm happy to put on a muumuu and cut up a pineapple and play Gabby Pahinui records, if you like."

She took his hand. "And I was hoping my mom could come visit sometime—I know it's a lot to ask."

It wasn't. He liked her mother, Marge. She lived in Wauwatosa and called Joyce every day and was weepy with Christmas coming on, remembering her late husband, Mutt, and how he loved his outdoor Christmas lights. James liked Marge okay.

But he and Joyce had had an argument about Marge a couple of months before, when Joyce was in the throes of PMS.

PMS hit Joyce harder than it did most women. She lay in the dark weeping and listening to Tchaikovsky and, in the throes of hormone poisoning, worked herself up into a state and thought that James wanted to go to Hawaii so as to avoid going to Wauwatosa to her mother's, whose Christmas lights he thought were garish and lower class. He had no such opinion! He had been careful not to form an opinion. The lights simply were what they were. He knew that in times of deep toxic PMS, he should show endless patience and kindness, and that particular night, she emerged red-eyed from the bedroom and said, "I've decided that we don't need to go to Mother's for the holidays. She's weird and depressing, and you get depressed enough by Christmas without her and her bubble lights adding to the problem."

Later, in retrospect, he knew he should have said, *I love your mother and I enjoy seeing her—at Christmas or any other time. She is a dear and good woman. I make no judgment about the bubble lights. Or the revolving Christmas tree stand that plays "O Tannenbaum." Let's not talk about it now, darling. Let's go to bed and I'll hold you in my arms and kiss your neck.*

What he actually said was "If that's what you'd like, fine. Maybe she has other plans."

She said, "Well, that's what you'd like, isn't it?"

"If that's what you want, darling," he said.

She said, "I remember how irritated you got with her last year when she talked about how she couldn't understand people objecting to Christmas trees in schools. You sat there grinding your teeth."

"I didn't grind my teeth, I simply disagreed with her on constitutional grounds."

"She has gone through so much and now she has her gluten problem . . ."

"I know—"

"To live your life knowing that if you walk past a bakery and inhale the exhaust, your throat could swell up and you'll have to dig in your purse for the emergency kit and before you can find it, maybe you're on the floor, clutching at your throat and gasping and people are stepping around you and averting their eyes—"

"Darling, invite your mother here if you want her to come."

And she sobbed that she didn't want her mother to come

where she wasn't wanted. "Please, don't," he said. She said that she was not about to throw away her flesh and blood as if they were garbage. "My mother is seventy-eight, and I'm supposed to—what? Throw her in the ditch? Because she's an inconvenience? She's my mom. And someday she's not going to be there anymore and I'm gonna miss her so much. And I'm going to feel terrible that I never gave her a grandchild." She blew her nose, *Breaughhhh*. "Oh James, is that why you refuse to give me a baby? The fear of heredity? That a baby would look like my mother?"

And she ran into the bedroom and locked herself in, and when he tapped on the door and begged her to come out, she said she needed to be alone right now.

And she emerged an hour later in her white bathrobe and apologized in a chill tone of voice and took a sleeping pill and went to sleep at nine o'clock. It sort of put a damper on the week.

But now that was over and they'd moved on, he thought, to post-PMS reasonableness, and he hoped to persuade her (rationally) that Kuhikuhikapapa'u'maumau would be beneficial for both of them. The sun was shining there. The mangoes and pineapple were fresh. They could be happy together! You don't need a tsunami of Christmas music and a truckload of gaudy gifts to be happy. A little warmth and sunshine are enough.

He wanted to tell her, *This pump-handle obsession has got me by the throat, babes. I keep imagining that I am standing in someone's backyard in Looseleaf with my tongue frozen to a pump and I am whimpering and nobody can hear me and I have to yank myself off the pump—it's driving me crazy. Have mercy, darling. Say you'll come to Kuhikuhikapapa'u'maumau.*

But he was afraid that if she knew how bunged-up he was and crippled by dread and shame, maybe she'd decide he wasn't worth sticking around for. Dump him and find someone normal.

7. A call from North Dakota

"I was reading an article about the danger of changing climate in midwinter," she said. "You go south in the winter, it makes you dreamy and you are liable to have something fall on you. This happened to my uncle Harley. He flew to Sarasota and stayed at a motel called Bright's Cabins, where the motel owner had put his anvil up in a tree so his wife wouldn't find out. He had bought it cheap, three hundred dollars for an eight-hundred-pound anvil, a good deal, but he had an anvil already, so he anticipated there would be questions. My uncle walked under that tree, though Mr. Bright had told him not to, and the anvil killed him flatter than a pancake and he was buried in a child's coffin, folded in two twice. It was warm weather that affected his thinking process. There was a man named Dobson from Wauwatosa who went to El Paso in February for the warmth and there in the bus depot, on pure impulse, he bought a nice-looking house in Mexico for five hundred dollars—the man had pictures of it, and Dobson paid him in cash and went to the ticket window to take a bus to Mexico to see the place and realized he didn't know what city or town it might be in and the man who sold it to him was gone like snow in July. Warm weather. Two days later he met a man in a café to discuss a business opportunity—a taxidermy business you could operate out of the trunk of your car and turn people's beloved dogs and cats into statues—and Mr. Dobson was thinking this over and his bowl of chili came and he stuck his fork in it and ate the plastic they put over the chili and choked on it and almost died. Warm weather affects the brain if you're not used to it."

The phone rang as Joyce was telling him about Mr. Dobson. It rang twice more as he begged her to keep an open mind about a Hawaiian vacation. She picked it up on the fifth ring. "It's Liz," she said.

"I don't want to talk to her," he whispered.

"Too late."

Liz was apologetic. "You're busy. I'm getting you at a bad time, aren't I? I can hear it. Listen, I'll send you a text message."

"It's okay. What's up? How's everybody?"

"It's nothing important, so don't get all het up."

"About what?"

"Listen—Jimmy, I can tell I've upset you. I'll call back when you settle down."

"What's going on?"

"So you didn't hear about Daddy?"

"What about Uncle Earl?"

"I shouldn't even say. He didn't want you to know."

"Know what?"

"It's nothing. He's old. Everything comes to an end eventually. There are no guarantees in life. We'll deal with it. You've got enough to worry about."

"Tell me what's going on, Liz."

"I shouldn't have said anything. He had to go into the hospital on Tuesday."

"What's wrong?"

"Daddy told me not to call you because he knew you'd be upset. I'm sorry I opened my big mouth."

James took the phone in his right hand and was about to whack the table with it and then he said, "Liz, if you don't tell me what's going on, I'm going to hang up and block your number."

Mrs. Sparrow got up from the table and whispered, "I have to go throw up now."

"What's wrong?" he said.

"Are you sitting down?" said Liz.

"Not talking to you. Talking to Joyce."

"It's only stomach flu," said Mrs. Sparrow.

"I think you should see a doctor," he said.

"He already did," said Liz. "Three of them."

"Talking to Joyce."

"His left eyeball fell out," said Liz.

"His eyeball fell out?"

Mrs. Sparrow put her hand to her mouth and gagged.

"It was only the left one. He was watching the Lawrence Welk Christmas special on TV and Bobby and Betty did a beautiful tap dance to 'O Holy Night' and Daddy got weepy and rubbed his eye and it just fell out. It was hanging by the optic nerve. He has skin cancer and it spread to his eyes. But they popped it right back in. He's fine. No problem. He didn't want me to call you and bother you."

"Oh my God."

"Anyway, could you call him and tell him a joke and cheer him up a little? You know he thinks the sun rises and sets on you, and he still talks about the time you flew out here for his birthday—when was that? Ten years ago? Anyway, you mean the world to him, and frankly—I shouldn't say this, but . . . I don't know as he'll make it to Christmas." And then she broke down and cried and hung up. Not like Liz to fall apart like that, she being a member of the National Rifle Association and a Republican and all.

8. A difficult decision

Looseleaf was fifty miles from Bismarck. There were five flights a day, Minneapolis to Bismarck. He should get on a plane and see Earl before cancer swept him away. He turned to Mrs. Sparrow. "My uncle Earl is dying. He has skin cancer and his left eyeball fell out. They think it's in the last stage."

"The happy uncle? The one who always made you laugh when you were growing up?"

"Yes. I'm thinking about flying up there today. I hate to leave you, but I ought to say good-bye while I can."

To fly to Bismarck and back cost $700. You could get economy standby fares to Hawaii for less than that. A fact to ponder.

Uncle Earl was the brightest penny in a handful of loose change. He was the cheerfullest man in Looseleaf, who every day did all he could to put a sunny smile on the gloomy windblown faces around him. He loved electricity, which shed light on life and saved men and women from backbreaking labor so they could live, love, laugh, and be happy. He was the superintendent of the county hydroelectric station, a spotless brick building alongside the Stanley River, and he believed in hydroelectric as God's gift to man and the cheapest and most reliable source of power. If someone's power went out in the middle of the night, Earl climbed into the Power Co-op truck and went off to repair the problem. He was a fixer-upper and a friend to all and he was James's salvation as a boy growing up in a desolate dusty town in an eternity of wheat and soybeans. He took James fishing summer mornings, early when the mists hung over the water of Lake Winnesissebigosh and recited Poe and Longfellow and Edgar Guest.

He was a cheerful optimist in a family of cranks and grumblers and mournful men and sour women with hound dog faces all aggrieved about money and cars and worried about kids poking their eyes out with sharp sticks and having to learn Braille or the baby eating fistfuls of toilet bowl cleanser, or Communists taking over, or a small plane crashing into the house, or the Christmas decorations strung above Main Street coming loose in a wind and fifty-pound angels falling down and killing someone. And of course the danger of Christmas tree fires. And there in this sinkhole of anxiety stood Uncle Earl, smiling, bow-tied, trim mustache, hair parted in the middle, and a carnation in his lapel, and if a priest walked by, or a blonde, or someone from

Minnesota, Earl had a joke for you, or two if you showed interest—and fresh ones, not the tired old jokes you'd heard before. Out of sheer goodwill, he was apt to break into "Kathleen Mavourneen" or "Five Foot Two, Eyes of Blue, Has Anybody Seen My Gal?" He carried gingersnaps with him that had a real snap to them, because ginger stimulates clear thinking. He'd make ginger ale punch and put on a record of the Mormon Tabernacle Choir singing:

> *By the old Moulmein Pagoda*
> *Looking eastward to the sea,*
> *There's a Burma girl a-settin'*
> *And I know she thinks of me.*
> *For the wind is in the palm trees,*
> *And the temple bells they say,*
> *"Come you back, you British soldier,*
> *Come you back to Mandalay."*

And the man and the boy stood and marched in time to the chorus, swinging their arms, and sang at the tops of their voices:

> *On the road to Mandalay,*
> *Where the flying fishes play,*
> *And the dawn comes up like thunder*
> *Out of China cross the bay.*

Earl had no enemies and held no grudges, and when a new county board was elected in 1953 on a platform of fighting Communist infiltration and decided to abandon hydroelectric for a giant diesel generator and took trips to New Orleans, Dallas, Las Vegas, and Phoenix to search for the proper generator, and in Tucson met a diesel salesman who took them out to a fine steakhouse and introduced them to three young women named Tammy, Bambi, and Trixie, and the next morning the board signed the contract, and the diesel was shipped to Looseleaf, the hydroelectric plant was shut down, and the diesel got hooked up and ran, more or less, for a couple of years, and the price of electrical power tripled, and Uncle Earl was fired and replaced by the brother-in-law of an anti-Communist, that didn't darken Earl's nature at all. He just opened a vegetable stand and sold watermelon, sweet corn, peppers, tomatoes, potatoes, and Swiss chard. And he told James, "Don't worry about the past and don't try to solve the future. Bravery and adventure! That's the ticket! Don't sit and gather moss. Get up, get out, do what you dream of doing, and if it doesn't work, it doesn't work, and you don't need to make that particular mistake again, but at least you won't get old wondering what if you had."

Like the Christmas Uncle Earl decided to experiment with candles on the Christmas tree. He had seen this in Victorian picture books, the master of the house lighting the candles and the children dazed with wonder, and so he

went ahead—secretly, of course; why spoil the surprise?—
and bought an eight-foot Norwegian pine and six dozen
clip-on candleholders and let Aunt Myrna hang the bulbs
and doodads and gewgaws and tinsel, and on Christmas Eve
he snuck out of the Methodist church during the singing of
"Silent Night" and trotted home and hung the candles and
then, when he glimpsed Myrna and the children and the
Sparrow family and Aunt Mona and Boo and Sherm heading for the house for the oyster stew and the cardamom
buns, he took a little gas torch and lit seventy-two candles
just in time for the whole gang to come piling in the front
door, but they made a beeline for the kitchen, not the living
room, where the astonishing thing stood in its flaming
glory, and when he cried, "Let's all go in the living room!"
nobody budged. So he cried out, "Let's open presents!" But
Myrna was already handing out cups of mulled wine. So, in
desperation, he yelled, "The tree's on fire!" And the whole
bunch mobbed into the living room and indeed it was, and
James's mother, who got there first, fainted at the sight and
landed on little Liz and broke her collarbone and she had to
be driven forty miles to a hospital, which put a crimp in the
evening. Aunt Myrna said to him, "How could you have
done such a thing and not have warned me?" But it was
Earl's way to do things impulsively, with great enthusiasm.
And thereby made an indelible Christmas memory for each
and all, and on succeeding Christmases the mere sight of a

cluster of candles brought it all back, the majesty and the terror of it.

When James was fourteen, Uncle Earl gave him a stuffed owl for Christmas, and the next year he wrapped up the owl and gave it back, and this became their Christmas tradition. "It's the thought that counts," said Uncle Earl. The owl's name was Howard and it had flown to San Francisco when James lived there and to Minneapolis and Kansas, back and forth between James and Looseleaf, North Dakota, getting a little more bedraggled every year from frequent fumigation, its beak and talons painted bright red. Last Christmas Mrs. Sparrow begged him to retire the bird. "It's gross," she said. "There's stuffing leaking out. The empty eye socket gives me the creeps." But James wrapped Howard up and mailed him off, and a week later Cousin Liz called to say the owl had not arrived.

"I sent it UPS."

"Hasn't come."

He tracked the shipment online. The owl, apparently, was being held in Minneapolis. There was a rule against shipping a dead carcass without labeling it as such. "It's only an owl," he said. The UPS agent promised to see what she could do. But Howard had disappeared for good. And now Uncle Earl was about to make his exit.

9. He flies through the storm into the land of dark memories

It was starting to snow when he left home and when he got to the airport the snow was coming down hard. It was two o'clock. The terminal was almost empty. He bought his ticket and tramped through security toting a backpack with a change of clothes and his shaving kit, and headed down Concourse C to the gate. His cell phone rang. It was Billy Jack, fit to be tied about an article in the *Mid-Atlantic Journal of Medicine* purporting to show that coyote grass is somehow tied to a loss of language skills. "I have no idea what my net worth is going to be Monday morning," he cried. "I am being crucified. I told the Boys' Club that I have to postpone my gift of a half million, and now the paper is barking up my tree about that. God!"

"I'm on a plane to Bismarck, sir. I'll be back on Monday and we'll deal with it. Don't worry yourself. These things blow over faster than a summer storm."

Billy Jack sputtered something about Midwesterners resenting the successful, and Mr. Sparrow suggested that he get out of town—maybe fly to Hawaii. Billy Jack seemed intrigued by the idea. "Worst thing you can do is talk to the press right now," said Mr. Sparrow, "and one good way to keep from doing that is to spend a week on the beach and sleep in a room near the surf."

"You're a man after my own heart, Sparrow," said the boss.

The plane to Bismarck was a small regional jet, a row of single seats on the port side, double seats on starboard, and the pilot in the left-hand seat was a slender woman with long blond hair. The flight attendant was a doughy-faced man named Jeff who did the safety briefing in a slurred voice, every word unintelligible. Mr. Sparrow fell asleep on the take-off and woke up as the plane was descending through a gray cloud bank, diving down, down, down, like a cage descending into a mine shaft, the cloud getting darker and thicker. And as he looked out the window into the murk, the memory of that old Christmas of the Great Flu came back to him. His humiliation in the snow. And the laughter from the neighbors next door—their old pump behind the garage, the handle loose, shaking in the wind, making a sort of low guttural chuckle.

The plane bucked in the clouds, and Jeff was making an announcement—Mr. Sparrow heard the words "if Bismarck is your final destination" and thought, *My God, no, no*—and then Jeff said, "We will be on the ground shortly" and

Mr. Sparrow felt a heaviness in his gut and imagined the smoking ruins of the aircraft smooshed against the prairie, and then the plane broke through a low ceiling—a few hundred feet—and down over snowy fields, a farmyard with six big blue silos, a windbreak row of poplars, a stretch of corn stubble, a county road with no traffic moving, and then down on the tarmac. The blonde put the brakes on hard and reversed the engines and they stopped in short order and turned sharply in toward the terminal, where he could see, through the falling snow, a few figures in parkas waiting beside a pickup truck, its hazard lights flashing.

The plane wheeled around to the terminal, bumping over the little drifts. A kid in blue coveralls came running out with the chocks and the jet bridge rolled up to the plane and Mr. Sparrow strolled into the terminal and there was his cousin-in-law Leo Wimmer, Liz's husband. With the furry hood around his face, and the snow falling, he looked like a last survivor of the Shackleton expedition. Liz had sent him.

"Hope you brought your pajamas," he said. "Forecast says there's a foot or more of snow on the way. Liz would've come but she had a little crisis. She came home from having four wisdom teeth pulled and was zonked on Vicodin and went upstairs to use the toilet and she pulled about a hundred yards of toilet paper off the roll, so the toilet overflowed and it was leaking through the dining room chandelier and dripping from the crystal beads and I can't get up on a ladder because my prostate is the size of a seedless orange and I'm due to go in for a ream job after the first of the year, so I left your cousin mopping up pee off the good rug and I go out to shovel out the car and I get hit by a snowmobile. Isn't that just the way it is?" And he clapped James on the back. "It's good to see you."

"Wish I were coming on a happier occasion than Uncle Earl being at death's door."

"Well, some days he is and others he isn't. I mean, everybody's at death's door if you want to look at it that way. But for many of us, the door is locked. If you get my drift." He didn't.

Leo's station wagon was in the parking lot, in snow up to its hubcaps. A lake of snow with fresh snow quickly erasing the tire tracks across it. Leo pulled out onto the highway, and James called Uncle Earl, who sounded pretty chipper for a dying man. "Remember that time the snowbanks were fifteen feet high and you and me had to shovel and throw the snow way up and our arms got tired?" said Uncle Earl. "And we tied clotheslines to our belts so if there was an avalanche they could pull us out in time? Remember that?"

"I thought you were sick, Uncle Earl."

"Ha! Some people wish I were! Not sick, just feeling a chill. I crawled into my nest here, piled up some quilts, and burrowed down like an old rat and was living on peanut butter cookies and water chestnuts, but now that you're here, I'm fine. When you coming over? Faye's tickled to death. She can't wait to see you."

His cousin Faye had recently moved back to Looseleaf after her husband, Floyd, kicked the bucket in Sedona, Arizona. She was a poet, a painter, and a professional storyteller. She hired herself out to public schools and went around in a beady dress and feathery hat and told ancient Ojibway myths such as "How the Muskrat Got His Name" and "Where the Snow Goes in Summer," though she was no more Ojibway than the Pope in Rome.

"You sound good, Uncle Earl," James said. "I heard you were in rough shape."

"Just waiting for spring. Waiting to hear the bluebirds sing."

"I heard you had skin cancer."

"When you're my age, Jimmy, you pick up all sorts of things, like a dog catches burrs. It comes with the territory. You're in the land of old age. Your prostate feels like a hockey puck and the people in obituaries look younger and younger and every time you go down the steps, someone is reaching for your elbow. They say, 'You're looking good.' Which they never said back when you did look good. All your friends are gone off to the desert—God knows why—and there's fewer and fewer to talk to about old times. Had a stroke a year ago and they raced me off to the hospital, though I was just fine—"

"A stroke? I never heard about that."

"It was nothing. They stripped off my clothes and ran me through the MRI machine for forty-five minutes of whanging and banging and buzzing and found that my heart had fired a blood clot up into my brain, into what neurologists call a 'silent' area of the brain, a part where not much is going on—sort of the North Dakota of the brain—and so nothing was affected, I could still talk a blue streak, but they kept me there for a whole week, climbing the walls, and the kids were talking about shoveling me into the Good Shepherd Home, but what kind of a deal is that for an old man? You've got to hang out with people you've been avoiding all your life and you're back on the hot lunch program you hated in grade school and you've got nothing to look forward to except the day they dress you up in the suit you used to wear to other people's funerals and put you in a box and haul you into church and you lie there and listen to somebody you barely know talk about your life, except he gets it all wrong, and then the pallbearers carry you out and they are of uneven height, so it's a rough ride, and into the black wagon you go thinking of all the car trips you were still planning to take and up the hill they take you and carry you out onto the frozen tundra and set you down on a brass frame and they sing a couple verses of 'Abide with me, fast falls the eventide' and somebody reads a prayer off an index card and everybody leaves. Your friends head for the saloon.

Nobody throws herself on your coffin and sobs and says she can't live without you. You lie there in the cold and then the gravediggers come over and you smell their cigarette smoke and wish they'd give you one and then down into the dark you go. That's what happens if you go into the Good Shepherd. So I'm staying at home for now. They got a very nice Indian lady to look after me."

Snow was falling and blowing sideways and Uncle Earl talked the whole time it took Leo to drive into Looseleaf. The snow was so heavy James could barely make out the red light on the water tower, the grain elevator by the train tracks, the old high school, and the bell tower of St. Margaret's Catholic Church. A grim-voiced announcer on the radio said that people should drive only if necessary and avoid the back roads. "If you get stuck or run off the road, turn on your hazard lights and hang a red flag from your radio antenna. Do not set out on foot. Remain in your vehicle. Conserve body heat by hugging each other. If this is not possible, use floor mats for insulation."

"This is North Dakota, for gosh sakes. I don't know what the big panic's all about," said Leo. "It's like nobody ever saw a snowstorm before."

Leo had a habit of slowing down and speeding up in a nervous rhythmic way. He reached for the radio dial—"Don't turn it off," said James. "I want to hear the weather."

"You can see the weather," said Leo.

The announcer was saying, "If you are stranded in a de-
serted area, stay with your car. When the wind lets up, spell
out the word H E L P in the snow and put rocks or tree limbs
in the letters to attract the attention of rescue airplanes. Be-
ware of hypothermia and frostbite. Breathe cold air through
your nose, not your mouth, so as not to frost your lungs.
And when you are around pump handles, railings, or other
iron objects outdoors, do not put your tongue on them or
your tongue will freeze to the object and rescuers may not
be able to hear your muffled cries for help until it is too
late."

"Pump handles!" cried Leo. "How ridiculous! Who's going to put their tongue on a pump handle?"

"People do strange things under stress. The human mind
is a complicated thing. You never know. Pump handles are
dangerous, I know that."

And then came the meaty voice of the governor saying
that everything that could be done was being done and that
he was monitoring the situation closely and people should
stay in their homes and remain calm.

James thought they were heading for Uncle Earl's house,
but then Leo turned left on Fillmore. Leo said, "I promised
Liz you'd come say hi." He drove into the whiteness, the
tires grumbling on the snow, and then stopped in the middle
of the street. "Got to warn you about Liz," he said. "She's on
a tear about Canadians. She listens to late-night radio out of

New Mexico and she heard that Canadian Intelligence—
CanTell, it's called—is slipping agents across the North Dakota border, and she's been driving around with a shotgun
looking for cross-country skiers. Liz gets a little excited
from time to time."

And then a man rapped on the window and it was Jack
Cobb from the old days. "Jimbo!" Boy oh boy. Jack reached in
the window and shook his hand. His breath smelled of dead
raccoons and rotten lumber. "What's new with you, Jimbo?
Thought you left a long time ago." Mr. Cobb laughed.
"Didja hear the one about the small town where the popula-
tion stays the same because every time a baby is born, a
man has to leave town?"

Leo chuckled. "Reminds me of the one about the man
and his wife who had twelve kids because they lived near
the train tracks and when the midnight train came through
and woke him up, he'd say, 'Well, should we go back to sleep
or what?' and she'd say, 'What—'"

Jack was opening the van door now. "Let's have a look at
you, for cripes' sake. You look like you could still go nine
innings, Jimbo. Nice coat. How much that set you back?" He
told a couple of Ole and Lena jokes and invited James to attend the lutefisk dinner at the Lutheran church and then they
got under way again. The snow was coming down in big
fluffy flakes like chicken feathers, and now Leo had lost track
of which way was west. He turned left onto a street that

didn't feel like the right way—a street that to James looked so familiar, and then it dawned on him: his street! His old street. Davis Avenue. And his boyhood home was up ahead on the right. The little white story-and-a-half frame house with the two oaks in the front yard.

He used to walk down that driveway to school and turn right to take the long way around and avoid the Durbins, who lived between his house and school and always were lying in wait for him. He used to shoot baskets in that driveway, back before the garage was brought down by carpenter ants. Come December and the Arctic blast, their old Ford coupe sat out in the open and froze to the gravel. Daddy put the key in the ignition and it was like trying to start a box of hammers. So he brought out a bucket of hot coals and put them under the engine block to warm up the crankcase oil to where it'd flow and then James got behind the wheel while Daddy pushed the Ford down the slight incline of the driveway and at just the exact right moment, James had to pop the clutch, and if he timed it exactly right, the momentum of the car turned over the engine and it fired up, and if he didn't do it right, the car jerked to a stop and Daddy had to call up Mr. Wick to come over with jumper cables, and to be beholden to Mr. Wick was something Daddy preferred to avoid. Mr. Wick was a Democrat and an agnostic, or the next thing to it.

He told Leo to slow down as they came to his old house, and Leo stopped. There was a new garage plus a deck where the old incinerator used to be, where he used to burn the trash, including aerosol cans that said DANGER: MAY EXPLODE IF EXPOSED TO OPEN FLAME. And the driveway where the old Ford coupe rolled slowly, creaking, little James hanging on to the wheel and peering out through a tiny aperture in the frost on the windshield, the car jolting over the bumps, bouncing like a wild bronco, the shock absorbers frozen solid, the boy hanging on to the wheel, his foot slipping off the gas pedal as Daddy cried, "Now! Now!" and trees going past while the boy hung on, and then he popped the clutch and the engine roared and the car jumped forward and he slammed on the brake and remembered to hit the clutch too, and the old Ford sat there, shaking, and Daddy opened the door and said, "Get out before you kill it."

And off he trudged to the bus stop, four-buckle overshoes crunching on the snow, a boy in a blizzard, unable to see more than a few feet ahead, hearing other children whimpering in the whiteness and the snarl of carnivorous dogs and the sound of sharp cracks that might be trees cracking or maybe the earth itself. A planet with hot molten rock in the middle, that is frozen solid at the top—something has to give. The earth cracks wide open and limbs fall off trees and pin you to the ground. Or maybe you walk across the snow and step into a bear trap. *Whack!* it breaks your leg. Or you step into a deep hole, and there's a bear in it, a bear who has eaten nothing but dirt and leaves for weeks and is ravenous.

Winter was a world of anxiety for young James. Bears, bear traps, trees falling, and then there was the fear of Communists. They could come skiing down from Canada, across an undefended border, and line the children up in the playground and give them a choice: either say "I hate America and I don't believe in God whatsoever" or else put your tongue on a frozen pump handle. What would he do then? He knew what he'd do, he'd renounce America and God, and the Communists would all clap and cheer, but God wouldn't like it at all, and in the next instant the boy would be in hell, flames licking at his feet, burning people walking by.

"What are you so quiet about?" said Leo.

"Thinking," he said. Thinking about Kuhikuhikapapa'u'-maumau and the fragrance of flowers on the breeze blowing through the lanai as he and Joyce strolled down to the beach to swim in the moonlight.

Leo stopped. "Where am I?" he said. James got out of the car and stood in the street, in the hush of snowfall. Nobody was out shoveling, everybody was sitting tight. The electric carillon at the Methodist church was playing "O Come, O Come, Emmanuel." The sermon on Sunday, according to the marquee, would be "Behold Him, O Ye Peoples." Whiteness glittering everywhere, the wind whipping up little eddies of snow on the drifts across the frozen tundra. The old house on the corner was Daryl Holmberg's and there was old Daryl in the living room, blue TV light flickering on his sleepy face: his old classmate, a Methodist deacon now, but back in the day he liked to torture smaller, nerdier boys and throw jagged iceballs at people. James's dad's friend Archie Pease, who lived across the street, wrote a column for the *Weekly Binder* ("Pease Porridge"), and next door was Rochelle Westendorp, the town librarian, who was mad at James for something he had said years ago. Something about women. And Paul Werberger, a bachelor who lived with four dogs and six cats and collected old magazines and played the banjo. And then James's aunt Mona's house was up ahead, a little cottage under a giant Norway pine, where she lived until Gene passed away and then she fled North Dakota for Ventura, California, and never was forgiven for it. Ventura was warm and sunny year-round, and she loved it there and never came back home to visit. So when she died, alone, happy, in her home on Catalpa Avenue, the relatives raised the money to fly her body back and bury it in the cold ground of Looseleaf, North Dakota. All alone, by the back fence. *Mona Sparrow, 1915–1998.*

10. A night on Lake Winnesissebigosh

A stiff wind out of the northwest whipped the snow across the prairie. According to the radio, two storms had converged. The curvature of the jet stream had flattened out and two storm fronts had intermixed. Airports across North Dakota were closing down. The eastbound Empire Builder had stopped in Montana and the westbound in St. Paul. The interstate was down to one lane in each direction.

He was going to be staying in Looseleaf for a while. No Hawaii for him. He had flown to North Dakota on the day he could've flown to Hawaii and that was the choice he had made. And now he was stuck here. And—God help us—he might very well be stuck until Uncle Earl died. It wouldn't be the quick, comforting visit he'd been planning, but a lengthy stay as Uncle Earl sank down, James sitting at the bedside, holding the old man's hand and—what? Saying the Lord's Prayer? Singing "Beautiful Isle of Somewhere"? He had never been in the presence of death before. What if he cracked under the strain? His uncle lying inert with an oxygen tube up his nose and his daughters sniffling in the room and Christmas music on the radio and the smell of medications and old man urine and Uncle Earl's rough breathing. And then his chest heaves and a long sigh and silence and Liz and Faye rise and approach the bed and burst out in raw sobs and throw their arms around James, crying, "Oh Daddy! Daddy! Don't leave us!" A thunderstorm of emotion. That's what scared him. His cousins wailing and flopping around in his arms, and what if James at that moment of wild grief lost control of his deep obsessive urges and walked out the door in search of a pump handle? It was all much too vivid in his mind.

"Leo," he said. "Uncle Earl said he's lying down for a nap, so I think I'd rather not go to the house right now and wake him up. And I'm thinking I'd like to be alone right now. You ever get that feeling? There's something I've never told the family and that is that I'm on antipsychotic medications and sometimes I hit a low spot and I just need to sleep for a while. Is Floyd's fish house still out on the lake? I thought I heard that Faye still has them tow it out on the ice every year."

"Still out there. I don't think anybody ever uses it."

"Could you take me there?"

"Liz is expecting you, you know."

"I realize that. Tell her I ran into an old friend and went off to have a drink."

Leo murmured something about Liz wanting to see him, but he turned the car toward the lake. "You understand, Leo. I just need to be alone." The thought appealed to him. Sleeping the night in a dead man's fish house. Why not? He just plain wasn't up for a bunch of grief and hand-holding tonight. And there are no pumps out on the lake.

And Leo swung left at the next corner and a minute later he was driving onto the vastness of Lake Winnesissebigosh, heading for the fish houses out toward the middle of the lake, a long string of them, ghostly in the falling snow. The ice was twenty-three inches thick, according to Leo, yet it gave off banging sounds like an underwater howitzer. James jumped. "It's nothing," Leo said. "Ice expands and contracts. Perfectly safe."

Leo drove up to a fish house with an electric Christmas star glimmering on the roof. "Faye left it on. She can see it from her bedroom window. Reminds her of Floyd. Floyd put the star up to help him navigate when he got drunk. He'd have a few belts at the bar and then he'd think about how mad Faye would be, so he'd head out across the ice blind drunk and the star would lead him to the shack and he'd crawl in and sleep it off."

"Well—" said James, his hand on the door handle, and Leo said, "Yeah. Getting late. Glad you made it. Want me to show you how to light the stove?"

"I've got it."

"Maybe I should wait and make sure it lights."

"I'll be fine."

"You sure?"

"Positive."

"Well, you've got your cell phone and you know our number."

James thanked him and got out of the car and Leo did a big U-turn and headed for shore and James stepped into Floyd's fish house, a small dim room, plywood floor with two holes to fish through, but nobody had drilled through the ice. An iron woodstove, a canvas chair, a small square table with cigarette burns on the edges, a broad plywood shelf built in on one side to lie down on, a rolled-up down-filled sleeping bag on it, and beneath it, a cupboard full of cooking utensils and fishing gear, a smaller shelf above with books in a row, paperbacks, mostly mysteries and thrillers. A woodbox full of birch logs, some oak. He balled up a newspaper from a stack and stuffed it in the stove and lit it and got some kindling going and put in a couple birch logs and the place started to warm right up. He found a pair of insulated boots and a parka behind the woodbox and slipped out of his city shoes and into the boots. Floyd's old hunting boots. They were a size large.

He stepped out the door and stood in the enormous silence of the snowfall and looked across the snowy drifts on the broad reach of ice toward the lights of Looseleaf, barely visible in the distance. He thought, *I am not afraid to be out here alone in a blizzard. Most men would be and I'm not. This is the beauty of an obsessive irrational fear like the one I've got. You focus on that and your other fears recede. Richard the Lionheart, who rode into ferocious battle, swinging his broadaxe, was terrified of spiders. General George S. Patton could not bear the sight of sheep. Lindbergh, flying the Atlantic solo in his little plane, was terrified of tall women. Genghis Khan rode horseback because he had a well-documented ant phobia.* So he, James Sparrow, had benefited from this silly obsession with pump handles that, shamefaced, he had consulted specialists about, trying to overcome it, but in fact his pump-handle obsession was a sort of magic that kept worse phobias at bay. He had never been a hypochondriac, never worried about plane crashes or prostate cancer, never agonized over the lack of purpose in his life. He had never suffered that fear of mortality that drove middle-aged men to have affairs with teenage waitresses. *Be thankful for your afflictions. Some of them may be assets in disguise.*

Soon his nose was running and he felt an ache in his chest from the cold air. *Breathe through your nose, not your mouth*, said Mother. So lovely was the night, he walked away from Floyd's fish house toward the other shacks on the ice and past them toward the shore. *Quite a day*, he thought. *You start out in your Minneapolis condo trying to convince your upchucking wife to take a trip to Hawaii and you wind*

up in an old wooden shack on a frozen lake in North Dakota.
The snow descended in a steady silent sound, a sort of white
hush. He walked almost to the bushy shore and then sensed
movement in the underbrush and a chill panic touched his
heart. He turned around and walked, walked, walked—
resisting the urge to run—to the shack with the Christmas
star and opened the door and went in. The fish house was
quite cozy. He dug into the cupboard and found a half-full
quart bottle of Paul Bunyan bourbon and a pint of peppermint schnapps, a few old *Playboy*s ("lissome lonesome Kelly
Jo, 23, lounges by the pool, sipping a cool limeade. 'Though
it was my first time, I was quite relaxed about posing nude,
having always felt that the body is a thing of beauty'"), a
copy of a John Sandford novel, *Lamprey* ("the tall angry
man hurtled past the line of patrons at the coffee shop including a child of three or four years old like a cougar going
for a snow rabbit and snarled, 'Gimme a java, toots,' at the
startled barista, an attractive woman of perhaps twenty-
four or twenty-five, and when an older woman behind him
said, 'Uh, there is a line here, sir,' he turned and shrieked,
'You dumbheads can eat weasel poop for all I care,' and
pulled out what appeared to be a .45 caliber pistol and fired
two shots *bam bam* through the woman's left breast, which
flopped bleeding from her blouse like a small wounded animal such as a weasel or pocket gopher"), which he tossed in
the fire, which flared up, and he opened the sleeping bag and

laid it across the shelf and was about to crawl in when he heard snuffling outdoors and opened the door and walked out and looked around and turned to go back in the shack and there, sitting motionless beside the shack, was a gray wolf in the light of the blue moon. His eyes were greenish-yellow and unblinking. His ears perked, his forelegs braced, his fur rippled. His tail lay curled and quite still.

James stopped in his tracks. A shock to see a wolf, but deep in his brain his old Scoutmaster Elmer told him that, faced with a hostile animal, you must face him squarely and not attempt to run. No panic, no sudden moves. Square your shoulders and plant your feet and calmly look over the wolf's head as if observing something beyond. So he did. The wolf was fifteen feet in front of him; the door of Floyd's fish house was about fifteen feet behind him. If the wolf charged him, he decided not to turn and run but to let out a bloodcurdling scream and crouch low and go for the beast's throat. He felt a knife in the pocket of the parka among the flotsam, the lengths of string, needle-nose pliers, duct tape, an empty snoose can, a Bic pen, some lead sinkers, scraps of paper. He opened the knife. The blade was dull, but it would do. He withdrew it slowly and held it in his right hand hanging loosely at his side. The wolf blinked. He had noticed. Good. A little zap of confusion in the animal's brain. James got himself ready to move—stroll purposefully to the door and open it and slip inside. He guessed the shack was nothing the wolf cared to be part of. Probably it smelled horrible to him, the stench of man and his beverages and his dreadful urine.

He was about to back up, taking short steps, maintaining his gaze, but then the wolf blinked again. The wolf looked him in the eye. It was a look of recognition. The animal was perfectly calm. He had been waiting for James to come. This was not happenstance. This was a personal encounter.

11. To his surprise, the wolf turns out to be someone he used to know quite well

"You don't smell horrible to me," said the wolf in a low, whispery voice. "I remember all those smells quite well. I was once a man myself, like you. I remember your smell very well. Vicks cough drops and Old Spice cologne and Pepsodent toothpaste."

"Who are you, sir?"

The wolf chuffed, clearing his throat. He wasn't used to speaking. "We used to camp out here overnight, we Boy Scouts. There on the shore. There were thirteen of us, all in one tent, and our Scoutmaster. It was hard, pounding tent pegs into frozen ground. We built a bonfire and cooked supper in the coals, hamburger and potatoes wrapped in tinfoil. We slept rolled up in army blankets. The moon was out and I remember seeing you get up to go out and pee. You were gone a long time and I was worried about you."

James was remembering now, how he walked away from the tent in the bluish moonlight and headed into the woods, not wanting anyone to see him peeing. He crossed the muskeg and a ridge and hiked down a ravine and found a secret place and extracted his penis from where it had shrunk into its burrow and hot piss shot out of him. A rather majestic twelve-foot arc. Steaming hot, and when it hit the snow it had turned to ice chips. And when he was done peeing and had written his name and "Fourscore and seven years ago" in the snow, he looked around and couldn't remember which way he had come from. Lost on a cold winter night due to excessive modesty.

The wolf glanced toward shore. "I left the tent and walked into the woods and miraculously I found you and I led you back." The wolf spoke, hardly moving his lips, his voice very soft. "I saved your life."

So it was Ralph. And they were standing on the spot where Ralph's canoe sank that chill October day in 1992.

James was living in San Francisco at the time, but he heard the whole story from Liz: how Ralph had gone out duck hunting in his green wooden canoe, his big rubber hip boots on, and the canoe tipped and he plunged into the chill water and the hip boots filled up with water and he sank and drowned. They dragged the lake for him and two days later his body floated to the surface and drifted toward shore.

Floyd found him. Floyd lifted the horrible mass of bloated flesh into his boat and laid his slicker over it and never went hunting again.

"How are you, Ralph?"

A silly question.

"I was a happy man with a sad life and you are a sad man with a happy life," he said. "Just for your information. You can put away the knife, James. You won't need it. I'm here to guide you, not attack you."

"I don't think I need a guide, Ralph. I'm doing okay on my own."

The wolf sneezed and then sneezed again. Or maybe it was laughter. He spoke slowly. "You are a frightened man and you live in vast ignorance. And now you've come to a place you never intended to be and there is more at stake here than you know."

James put the knife away. "Do you mind if we step inside?" he said. And the door to the shack swung open.

He put another birch log on the fire and got down a cup and poured whiskey in it.

"Thank you for saving my life. I'd forgotten. I remember how horrible I felt when you drowned. What happened?"

"I was hunting, wading through the cattails, and I shot two ducks with two shots and they plunged into the water a hundred yards from shore. I could see them out there flapping and I got in my canoe to put them out of their misery.

86

My old retriever Jackson had died in March and I grieved for him and it took me a while to get myself a pup, and by the time hunting season rolled around, he wasn't trained in, so I had to retrieve the birds myself."

"I remember, you always hunted alone."

"I did. I liked my friends well enough, but I didn't go in for drinking in a duck blind and the bad jokes and the loud talk. They didn't care if they got game or not. I did. That was the point of it. I loved hunting. It wasn't about killing things; it was about the intense awareness when you sit perfectly still with eyes sharpened, nose to the wind, ears open, your whole being at attention. I feel this even more keenly as a wolf. A wolf can sit for hours of keen attention, hearing every whisper and trickle, every bird chitter and fish splash, the drip of rain, the hush of twilight, the raccoons washing their paws, the little fox learning to make no sound, and we wolves don't spoil the moment with a lot of yikyak about the sorrow of growing old. Hunting is sacred: why else would you sit there in the cold and damp? It's all about that awakening of the visceral senses that get dull in the ordinary dry tedium of indoor paper-pushing and the meetings and the sucking up to big shots, and now that I'm a wolf I am free of all that. I loved that dog of mine and now I am living his life. He was killed by a car that didn't bother to stop. It broke my heart, the cruelty of man, racing around with terrible force, heedless of what he destroys. So when those ducks splashed down, my heart felt torn in two, and I paddled out from shore in blind grief, and I grabbed one duck and reached for the other and it squawked and flapped away, mortally wounded, and I wanted to end its pain and I swung at it with the paddle, broke its neck, and myself plunged overboard and I sank quickly, my heart full of regret for Theresa, and I managed to get one hip boot off but not the other, and I sank to the bottom into the mud down beside some turtles and when I awoke, it was dark and I was surrounded by furry things who were snuggling up next to me. I was in a beaver hut. An extended family of beavers, and they brought me bark and moss and lily pads and I slept and slept and when I awoke, it was spring."

"What happened then?" said James.

"I worked in a Denny's in Fargo for a few weeks, clearing tables, bussing dishes. And nobody spoke to me ever, though I kept asking them why I was there, and that's how I knew I was dead. Because I didn't exist. And I wasn't paid a penny. And one night a woman came and sat in a back booth and asked me to bring her a bowl of rice and beans. I told her I was only a busboy. She wore a blue suit with a gold badge that said ATF and she was frightening to behold but beautiful. She said, 'Your old life is done and now you must begin the new one. You will spend a time grieving and treading the paths of your old life and seeing it with clear eyes, and then something else will happen.' And she waved a hand in my direction and I became as you see me, a gray wolf. And so I have lived in the creek bed where we used to camp, observing my people, whom I dearly loved, and who, though they are foolish, wasteful, of limited intelligence, and habitually cruel, I now love even more tenderly."

The wolf came over to James and lay his head on James's leg and said, "Every year during the Christmas moon, I have the power of speech and this is only the second time I've used it."

"What was the first?"

"I told Theresa that I loved her. She was horrified and slammed the door in my face."

The wolf's eyes filled with tears. "I didn't choose to leave the world and even now, years later, there are times I want to return. And Christmas is one of those times. Christmas and baseball season and the last week of August for the State Fair and the week in April when the blossoms open up."

"I never cared for Christmas," said James.

"I know all about that. And I don't know that it can be changed, though your rejection of Christmas will bring you terrible regret."

"What will I regret?"

"I'm not free to say. I can't tell you everything I know."

And then James had a fearful thought.

"Ralph," he said. "Tell me. Have I died and landed in hell? Will I be here forever? Is this going to be perpetual winter? Is this it, Ralph? Is this all there is?" But the wolf was gone.

He opened the door and saw a flicker of tail in the underbrush. "Ralph!" he called. *"Ralph!"* But he was gone.

And then he heard girlish voices counting off one-two-one-two-three and there were Debbie and Becky and Ginny and Joni and Julie and Nanci and Lori and Gloria, the Looseleaf cheerleaders in their scarlet-and-gray middie uniforms and long socks and sneakers and pom-poms in hand and singing the old school song:

> *We're here to fight for Looseleaf*
> *To the crimson team we're true.*
> *You can cry and howl, and throw in the towel*
> *Cause we'll tromp all over you (YOU BETCHA!)*
> *We're going to win for Looseleaf*
> *As you know darned well.*
> *We are the Lucifers, the mighty mighty Lucifers,*
> *And you can burn in hell. SSSSSSSSSSSS.*

They were seventeen and eighteen years old but their eyes were much older, and when he called to them, they looked his way without recognition, and when he said their names, they hissed at him, *Sssssssssssssss.* And then trotted off into the colony of fishing shacks and vanished.

He stood on the ice outside Floyd's fish house in a blind

panic. Maybe this world was trying to tell him it no longer wanted him in it and maybe a flight to Hawaii had been his one and only chance for survival and maybe his decision to come here and bid a dying uncle good-bye was a sort of death wish. He was alone on a frozen lake in a snowstorm with only a little wood to keep him from freezing to death.

He could die here and never see his dear Joyce ever again. She would grieve for six months or a year and then sell the condo and move to a new one and start dating men she'd meet online and eventually find one she liked and move in with him. A man who loved Christmas as much as she did. And one Christmas she'd tell her new lover about her late husband who disappeared in North Dakota and how much he loathed the holiday, especially "The Little Drummer Boy," and the two of them would laugh. Sitting on a nice sofa in an apartment in downtown Minneapolis, arms around each other, Joyce and What's His Name would laugh at the memory of that odd fellow James Sparrow. He worked for a company called Coyote Corp. and he hated Christmas. That would be his entire legacy.

12. In the terminal zone

He needed to settle himself down, so he sang:

On the road to Mandalay
Where the flying fishes play
And the dawn comes up like thunder
Out of China cross the bay.

But Mandalay was nowhere around here. He returned to the fishing shack with a heavy heart and when he opened the door, he was in a vast room in an airport, a room as big as three 747 hangars, and over the loudspeakers came a man's voice making important unintelligible announcements. James was standing in a long line of travelers waiting to speak to a woman with big black enameled hair who sat on a high stool behind a counter under a sign, EXTERNAL TRAVEL. She had several yellow pencils stuck in her hair and also a small telephone on a wire that went to a bud in her ear. She had very serious arched eyebrows.

The line was not moving. The man at the head of the line

was speaking to her and sobbing, and she looked at him impassively. He dabbed at his eyes with a hanky. He held out his arms, beseeching her, and she waved him away. The line inched forward. Next in line was a family, a woman and man and a little girl, and they had a long story to tell—it went on and on and on—and they were dismissed eventually, and then the woman behind them stepped forward and pulled out a violin and took her time tuning it and set up a music stand and a score and started to play. James said to the man in front of him, "Don't these people realize there are others waiting in line behind them?"

The man turned around and said, "وي‌ذهب ال‌عمر ض‌ع‌بل كون نحدودا. القلب ما ال تظار"

"I'm sorry. Could you speak English?"

The man looked as if he'd been at the airport for days or weeks. Dark circles under his soft brown eyes. Dark stubble on his cheeks and jaw. A white shirt, open at the neck, rumpled. Black hair, gray at the temples.

"I hope we won't have to wait too long, that's all," said James.

The man touched his arm. "يمكن ان نهاية واهن ال ينبغي وضعها في صندوق لك شخص هو مقدس واتي ال." he said.

It took some time to reach the front of the line, during which James lay down on the marble floor and slept and dreamed about Boy Scouts and standing in a straight line with neckerchief tight, back straight, saluting, as the bugler played Taps, and then the man behind him kicked him and woke him up and he scootched forward and slept some more and was kicked and inched forward and kicked and inched, meanwhile dreaming about the tall grass, the precipice, the sharks in the black abyss below, the buzzards circling, and finally he was the second person in line—the man in front of him pleading to go to Minneapolis where his beloved daughter was waiting for him, she needed him, she loved him, he was her daddy, her precious daddy, but it was no soap, Big-Hair Lady sneered and shook her head, withdrew a pencil, scratched his name off the list. The man slumped down sobbing about the unfairness of it, and then it was James's turn.

"I wish to go to Minneapolis. Or to Looseleaf, North Dakota. I seem to have jumped the tracks of my life and I'm in some strange void and I'd like to get back to my beloved wife and—I don't care about Hawaii—just want to see Joyce and get my life back. The familiar life. Okay?"

"Let me see your identification."

Well, of course he didn't have any. "I must've left it in my coat."

She was not interested in the idea of his not having identification. It didn't interest her in the slightest.

"Please," he said. "I'm a good guy. I'm a human being. Give me a break."

He might as well have said, "I am the ghost of William

Tecumseh Sherman" or "I am a man who uses proper grammar" or "I represent the oppressed of the world." Not of interest, sir.

"My name is James Sparrow and I live in Minneapolis with my wife, Joyce. I am employed by Coyote Corp., makers of an energy drink. I am forty-two years old and I am perfectly happy to go back so that I can celebrate Christmas."

She laughed a harsh, metallic laugh like skillets clanging—"You? Celebrate Christmas? That'd be like a sheep dancing the schottische. Like a hawk writing a haiku. Be serious, sir."

"My wife is ill. I want to be with her for Christmas."

"Your wife is sick of you, is the problem."

"Please," he said. "It would mean so much—"

Big-Hair Lady threw back her head and screeched.

"HA!!!" She shook her head. "Mister Sparrow, it would mean nothing to you. *Zero. Zilch. Nil. Ixnay.* You, sir, derive less real pleasure from this world than anybody who's ever come through here. You are blind and deaf and cold to the touch and you have no taste, and music and poetry and good cooking are lost on you. You're all tied up in knots about money and getting old and the daily insult of the bathroom mirror. You walk down city streets with no eye for your fellow citizens. You are offered magnificent music and you exit early so you won't get caught in traffic. You think happiness is somewhere out in the future but you have no more idea what it is than you could explain radioactivity. You are a man of stunning ineptitude. Your daddy knew about engines, plumbing, hydraulics, and arc welding and pouring concrete, gutting a deer, cleaning a walleye, digging a fish hook out of your thumb, not to get rich but just to get by, and here you are and you feel superior to him and you can't pour piss out of a boot when the instructions are printed on the sole. You walk through life like you're waiting for it to begin any day now. And it's almost over."

"Please, I'll do better." *Almost over?* What did she mean?

"Couldn't hardly do worse," she muttered, and scratched his name off the list. "I'm giving you twenty-four hours to go look around and make your peace. Go. Git. Scram. Out of my sight. And blow your nose, please."

He turned and ran out the door under the exit sign and there he was, back on the ice outside Floyd's fishing shack.

The stars shone in the sky, the other shacks were where they had been, the wind blew a little colder than before. He'd left the mittens and the parka back there in the giant terminal, and the wind was hard and sharp. He didn't dare go back for them lest the Big-Hair Lady revoke his pass. He stood on the ice, frozen between Forward and Reverse, and was starting to consider the option of freezing to death, when someone called his name. It was his cousin Liz.

13. James's inner resolve is sorely tested in the dark waters

"James, what the hell you doing out here?" He stepped toward her to give her a hug and warm up a little, and she didn't hug him back much; it was mostly him hugging her. She was lean, wiry, a cross-country skier who liked to ski in snowstorms. Once, trapped in a storm, she dug a hole in a deep drift and stayed there for four days, wrapped in a thermal sheet like tinfoil, and was able, she claimed, to lower her heart rate and respiration to something like a state of hibernation and thus conserve her strength. A true North Dakota woman.

"Leo said you insisted on coming out and staying in Floyd's shack so I came to make sure you've got a decent sleeping bag." She walked over to the shack. He took a deep breath and opened the door— and did not disappear into the Other World: no Big Hair there, just the lantern and stove and the cupboard with the sleeping bag on it—and she shut the door with a bang.

"Looks like you're all set," she said. She looked him up and down. "Kind of cold to go out without a coat," she said. "Come on over to my shack, I'm just starting a fire." Her shack stood closer to shore, an eight-by-ten structure of weather-beaten barn boards, smoke curling up from the stack. The woodpile next to it stood shoulder high. On the shack he could see several signs, EXTREMISM IN THE DEFENSE OF LIBERTY IS NO VICE and WHEN I HEAR THE WORDS GUN CONTROL I REACH FOR MY REVOLVER and NOW IS THE TIME FOR THE TREE OF LIBERTY TO BE WATERED WITH THE BLOOD OF TYRANTS.

Liz was a rabid Republican who believed that the U.S. government had secret agents on her trail, surveilling her with security cameras and satellites, ready to pounce at any time. She owned a steel helmet that deflected satellite rays, and carried two loaded .45 pistols in her yellow down vest.

Her house was kept hermetically sealed against bacteria that government agents might spray on the homes of patri-ots. She was a contributing editor of *Freedom* magazine and a leader of the citizen militia Possum Comatosis. She used Coy-ote and got along on two hours of sleep a night, a watchful sentry on freedom's ramparts. He liked Liz. He had always liked her since they were kids and played Three Musketeers in the court of Louis XIV of France and went swashbuckling around and being French, dueling with infidels—"Do me the honor, my good lord, of taking your sword from its scabbard," she cried and crossed swords with a phantom enemy and drove him down into the creek, where he slashed her face, *Mon Dieu!* And she dropped her sword and sank to her knees in abject pain. And then snatched up the sword and drove it through the blackguard's heart. *Allons!* "Long live the king." And now she was still caught up in swashbuckling, except against the government of the United States.

She opened the door to her shack and he walked in. It was dark except for the red glow from the firebox. At one end was a bench on an elevated platform. No fishing holes in the ice. And then he noticed, atop the firebox, a steel tray with rocks on it.

"I worry about you living down in Minneapolis and reading the mainstream press, James. You miss out on a lot." Liz believed that government is a relentless force seeking to imprison us in regulation, and any person with a brain fights back, but Democrats, like the majority of people, are lazy thinkers and in the end, some sort of armed uprising may be necessary to rescue the country from the tyranny brought on by the election of a foreign-born Muslim, Obama bin Laden, to the presidency.

"Minneapolis isn't all bad. This town doesn't hold a lot of wonderful memories for me, Liz. This town gave me permanent nightmares and put me into therapy."

"What you in therapy for?"

He made the mistake of telling her. Pump handles.

"Oh you're not one of those, are you?"

He was, actually. He was winter disabled. Some people had frost phobia or wind-chill anxiety. He had a pump-handle obsession. He tried to explain it to her, his powerful compulsion to put his tongue on an iron pump handle, even knowing that the tongue would freeze to the iron instantly and he'd either have to wait for help to arrive—some Good Samaritan: "What's wrong, sir?" *Mmmpfl rmnllglgl shrdll-rgrgr.* "I'm sorry, sir, I can't understand you"—so you count to three and pull away violently and rip the skin off. And that was why he lived in Minneapolis and avoided small towns during winter months and salvage yards and playgrounds and he longed to fly to Hawaii.

"And I'm seeing a therapist," he said. "In fact, several of them."

"Listen, James. No jerk in an office with a bunch of certificates on the wall is going to talk you out of belief in your own demons. You got to face them yourself." Her daughter Angie was in treatment for recovery addiction, Liz said. Angie liked to drink, so she went to AA because her boyfriend told her to and then she got to liking AA and went to different groups at different times of day and soon was up to twenty-one AA sessions a week, three a day, and was trying to cut down, and had joined an Addiction Recovery Dependency group.

Liz went outdoors and got an armload of wood and came back in and said she wasn't going to let him leave town until they had dealt with this pump-handle thing.

"I'm dealing with it."

"You're not dealing with it. I'm family, James. I can tell you things other people can't. You're full of BS and you need to clean out your system, and that's what we're going to do now."

"I don't know what you're talking about."

She grabbed a shovel from the wall and went outside and he followed—she walked over to a big rectangle cut in the ice and started punching at the thin ice that had frozen over it. And then she turned to him and told him to take his clothes off and follow her into the sauna.

"Aha," he said. And she grabbed the zipper on her big insulated jumpsuit and pulled it from her neck down to her left ankle and stepped out onto the ice naked. His cousin Liz. Her left breast was missing. Just scar tissue. "I had it cut off," she said. "It got in my way when I aimed a rifle."

She opened the shack door and now billows of steam came blowing out, and in she went. He stepped out of his boots and took off his shirt and pants and stood barefoot on the ice, a strong sensation, pain and then numbness, and a moment of decision: *Yes. No. Stay. Go.* And his life seemed to hang in the balance—a wrong move could lead to oblivion. *Why am I standing here? I have a life, a wife whom I love. I don't need this at all.* A man in his jockey shorts in a stiff wind. *What is this leading to? Run! Beat it! Scram! Get out of here!* This woman could eat you for breakfast. And then he stripped his shorts off and walked to the door. *I am a prisoner here and I am not going to give her the satisfaction of seeing me beg for mercy. For the honor of liberals everywhere*—he opened the door and stepped into a cloud of steam in pitch-blackness and closed the door. It was hot in there. Hotter than hot. It scorched his face. *Damn, it is hot.* He took a shallow breath. He could see her pale form sitting on the bench, and on the firebox, the rocks glowed, red-hot coals. A pail alongside. "Throw some water on," she said. He picked up the pail and sloshed water on the rocks. "Not so much." He was about to say sorry and caught himself. "In Minneapolis," he said, "we like a wet sauna. But whatever you like, Liz."

"Oh," she said. "Dry saunas a person can tolerate longer, that's all."

And in that moment, he knew he could best her. The tone in her voice. She'd expected him to come whimpering and cringing into her torture chamber, and he'd come marching in as a veteran, welcoming punishment.

"Wet saunas are more intense, but when in Rome—"

He plopped down beside her.

"Want a towel?" she said.

"Don't need one." He could hardly breathe. He didn't know how long he could sit here before his body burst into flame, but he was going to sit still right up to the moment of combustion. "This is great," he said. Sweat poured from him, salt stung his eyes. He wanted to weep for pain.

"Glad you like it." There was defeat in her voice. It thrilled him. Her hair hung limp on her bare shoulders, she was hunched forward—and then he saw the birch boughs on the bench beside him.

"Ready for some stimulation?"

She started to turn around and he grabbed the boughs and lashed her four, five, ten times, fairly hard. "Hard enough?" he said. "Or do you like it more brisk?"

"That's fine," she said. So he lashed her harder. It felt good. He hit her on behalf of Hubert Humphrey, Jimmy Carter, Walter Mondale, and Michael Dukakis, and she trembled. "Too hard?" he cried. "No," she whimpered. He lashed her good until she cried out, "Thank you. How about you?" and then he jumped up and said, "Time for a swim!" and out the door he went. Steam poured off him in the cold air and pure red-blooded Triumph was in his heart, and what is physical pain compared to Triumph? The freezing air blazed on his skin. He strode toward the big dark hole, Liz following a few steps behind him. His body was screaming at him, *Don't do this! We don't like this! Bad idea! Bad idea!*, but in his heart he knew he was right: *Show No Weakness!*

No Indecision! He turned toward Liz and she put an arm over her one breast and a hand over her crotch. "This is great!" he cried. "How did you know I love saunas?" And he turned toward the hole with the same holy devotion as the Christian martyrs stepped into the arena—*All or Nothing!*—and took three quick steps and launched out—*Lord Jesus Christ into Thy Hands I commend my spirit*—into the cold blackness and it shocked him like a sledgehammer—but not in a bad way! No no no—his skin was freezing and his teeth chattered but the core of him was hot, and between the two sensations was a center of equilibrium of pure feeling and high happiness, and he yelled, "It's great! It's beautiful!" which made her hesitate. She stood naked in the twilight, vulnerable and defeated, and he cried, "Thank you, Jesus! Washed in the blood of the Lamb! Hallelujah!" She thought he was crazy. *Good.* He whooped and yelled some more. She was steeling herself to jump but she had lost her momentum, and then he put his hands on the ice and hoisted himself up and stood and hugged her, and she almost collapsed from the shock. Her thin, trembling body in his grasp. "Praise God from Whom all blessings flow," he said and he threw her into the water. She let out a pitiful *Eeeek*, and he turned away and went into the shack. He put a fresh log on the fire and tossed water on the stones. She was right. He'd needed a break-through and he had broken through. He was all over the pump-handle business. Cured. He had stepped through that door and into the next room, which was beautiful and lumi-nous and shimmering with delicate delights, and in that moment he longed for his dear darling wife and wished she were in his arms, her strong shoulders, her broad naked back, her long legs, her sweet face turned up toward his, her Roman nose, and her dark hair pulled back, her smile, he wanted to kiss her smile and inhale her sweet voice.

14. Awakening to a new morning, he starts to feel at peace with the world

He lay down to sleep in Floyd's shack and drifted off amid feelings of transcendence and arose at dawn and put a couple of logs on the fire, and cut a hole in the ice and dropped a line in, bobber floating in the water, thinking that a walleye might be a good omen at this time, and made tea. He did his stretching exercises. He wanted to call Joyce and tell her he was cured of anxiety now, but it was only 6:00 a.m. She had left him a message on voice mail last night. Her calm and delicate voice. "I just called to say that I am missing you tons and tons and still feeling sort of under the weather and, speaking of weather, it looks like flying to Kuhikuhikapapa'u'maumau is out of the question anyway, and I hope you'll come back soon and we can have a beautiful Christmas, and I love you. I love you so much."

He was hungry so he threw on Floyd's parka and headed for town across the ice, walking briskly through the falling snow, a new man now, and he wondered if the Big-Hair Woman was going to come after him tonight or if the jump in the lake had maybe won his release from her powers. He wasn't sure. He walked up on shore and down the street where the Thackers lived and the Enghs, but there were new names on the mailboxes now, Gant and LaFever. Nobody he knew. The name of Sparrow had vanished, too. Brother Benny hanging on in Alaska, running a camera shop, and Elaine, sad, worn down, alcoholic, in Fort Wayne, two victims of loser romances, bad habits, and no luck whatsoever, and meanwhile their big brother, on the verge of falling off the edge of the world and into the black abyss of afterlife, had been given another chance. Unfair.

He walked in the Bon Ton Café, stomped the snow off his boots, and parked himself at the counter, feeling mightily empowered. He was cured of his Hawaiian longings, the dream of the shining beach and the white surf. He was not done with North Dakota yet. An old man stood peering out the big window. "This isn't over yet," he said. "We're gonna see a lot more of this before it's over. Where you come in from?"

"Minneapolis."

"You gotta be lost."

James shrugged.

"Not as bad as the storm of '75. That was a bad one. January. Roads were closed for eleven days. Eleven. Thirty-foot drifts. Empire Builder train got stuck thirty miles west of Minot and it took a week to dig those people out. There were children conceived on that train, that's how bad it was. Eighty-mile-per-hour winds, thirty-five died in North Dakota alone, and you know something? Most of them were glad to go. That's how bad it was." He took a sip of coffee. "Coffee's cold, Myrt." The waitress took a carafe off the hot plate and brought it over.

"I remember it well. Right here in town, a man and a woman were struggling through the storm to get home and finally they made it into the house and she looked at him and she'd never seen him before in her life. She said, 'You're not Bob.' He said no, he was Larry. She said, 'Where'd my husband go?' He said he didn't know, that he saw her alone in the storm so he joined her. She said, 'I wonder what happened to Bob. He never disappeared like this before.' She said, 'Well, as long as you're here, you may as well come in and get warm.' And he did. And they're still together. Had three children. Bob never came home. That was in 1975. January. Sure tells you something about marriage, doesn't it?"

The wind whistled in the weather stripping, just like it did in their house when he was a kid. Cold drafts. Once, Daddy woke up in the night, deaf in his left ear—it had been frozen by a cold draft. Never could hear in that ear again.

A man in a snowmobile suit sat on a stool at the counter

and Myrt slid a cup in front of him and filled it with java from the carafe in her right hand.

"You take cream, Bobby?"

"You know me better than that, Myrt."

"Oh yeah. It's your brother who takes cream. How's he doing in Florida?"

"He's stuck there, that's what. Paid three-quarters of a million for a house that's now worth about half that and he lost his job and he's working part time as a security guard."

"You ever been to Florida?"

"Why would I want to go there?"

"It's warm there."

"If you're cold, put on a sweater. That's what I say."

"I've got two on already."

The snowmobile suit and the waitress glanced over at James, sizing him up, trying to figure out what he was about. People in Looseleaf weren't what you'd call friendly. Strangers come in and Looseleafers look at you like they think they may have seen you on a Wanted poster at the post office and they're trying to remember if it was for homicide or larceny.

The snowmobile guy ordered a Western omelet and Texas toast. "You see that black BMW came into town yesterday?" he said. She shook her head. "Four people in expensive ski clothes heading for Sun Valley. Pulled into the

Pure Oil station and filled up with gas and then they drove around to the back and drove into the automatic car wash, forgetting the ski rack and the skis on the roof of the car."

"Oh my gosh."

"Yeah, those big overhead rollers grabbed the front tips of those skis and played them like a marimba and the driver was trying to back up and the others were screaming and the skis got ripped off and then the overhead got tangled up with the ski rack and it lifted the front end of the car up and shook it and one guy jumped out just in time to get waxed, and finally Stan found the Off button for the car-wash and let me tell you, that BMW needed its interior cleaned out—those folks had shit their pants. I'm not kidding you, Myrt. Stan brought them a bucket of soapy water and a green garbage bag and left them alone in there and they put their clothes in that bag and left it and he took it home and threw the clothes in the washer and now he's got some Swiss designer ski outfits, except they're too small for him."

He glanced over at James to see if he was paying attention. James looked straight ahead. He knew the type. The small-town storyteller. Another variety of braggart. The stories always had a victim, and it never was the storyteller himself, usually an outsider.

"So you're not moving to Florida, I take it?" said the waitress, bringing the Western omelet.

"No reason to go. There's no ice fishing down there."

"I could live without ice fishing. Nothing but an excuse to drink, if you ask me."

"Man has to keep off the chill any way he can."

"My brother never drank at home. A cocktail was foreign to Marvin, strange as an artichoke, but he'd go ice fishing, and when they passed the Four Roses he took a hit off it. And that was when he ran off with that woman. She was lost, or so she said, and came out to the fish house to get warm, and he warmed her up all right. Took her off to a motel and turned the heat up. And it all started with taking a drink."

"I never knew your brother, but I do know that a lot of people have perished in winter storms for want of a little whiskey. The death toll among Baptists is staggering."

"The woman he ran off with was a Baptist. Or married to a Baptist."

"Well, there's your motivation right there."

"I forget—did you say you wanted cream in your coffee?"

"Get away from me with that cream pitcher, Myrt."

The old man who was an authority on winter had moved over to the counter to get away from drafts. He motioned to Myrt for another cup of coffee. "Gimme the usual." He looked over toward James. "Man's got to keep up his strength in cold weather. Back in 1957 the temperature dropped forty degrees in one minute. Went from thirty-two to eight below. Sixteen teenagers were taken to the hospital. No scarf, no mittens, no warm jacket. Same winter we got ten feet of snow and a dozen houses collapsed from the weight on the roofs."

The snowmobile guy took the floor back, talking while he devoured his omelet. "My brother's father-in-law got talked into moving to Florida by his wife and it threw his immune system out of whack. He caught a virus that wouldn't go away and wound up in a hospital in Sarasota inside a plastic bubble with tubes running in and out and he lost a lot of brain function until he forgot his own name and birth date and he was transferred to a nursing facility, which actually was a warehouse full of people in containers, semi-comatose, all of them Midwesterners, snowbirds. Big sturdy people, farmers, brought down by climate-related illness, and they were kept alive so their organs could be harvested—eyeballs, bone marrow, a kidney, skin, whatever was needed—organs sold in Florida on the black market. He got his father-in-law out of there and put him in a regular nursing home and they ran out of money and had to give him over to the county and I don't know what happened after that except that my brother can't wait to leave Florida, but now he's become de-acclimated to cold weather and he's afraid he'd die if he came back. Caught between a rock and a hard place."

James called the Bismarck airport. A recorded announce-ment said the airport was closed, the runways were iced over, visibility a hundred feet. Nothing to do but sit tight. He called up Joyce and got her voice mail. "It's okay about Hawaii, darling," he said. "Kuhikuhikapapa'u'maumau will still be there whenever we want to go back."

At the mention of Kuhikuhikapapa'u'maumau, Myrt, Bobby, and the old man looked straight at him and you could see the question forming in balloons over their heads—*Who is he and what did he just say?*—but they didn't ask. That was Looseleaf for you. Stoicism, through and through, to the point of stupidity. No surprise, no alarm. Act like it's nothing. Blizzard, robbery, major coronary—*hey, no problem. Everything's under control.*

And then his phone rang. A local number. He had a hunch who it might be and he didn't want to talk to her, but he had been given twenty-four hours to make his peace and he intended to do that. He opened the phone. "Hi, Faye," he said. "How's tricks?"

"Jimmy," she said. "I've been up for hours saying empowering prayers for you and lighting Shoshone vision sticks. Liz called me at 4:00 a.m. and said you are suicidal. She said you stripped off your clothes and jumped into the lake and she had to dive in and pull you out. What is going on? I love you. We all love you and we support your journey, wherever it may lead, but don't choose the Death Mother, Jimmy. Don't embrace the Great Bear of Icy Solitude. If there's anything we can do to help you return to your deeper self you only need ask. I am so very, very happy you felt free to use Floyd's fishing shack, Jimmy. It was his spirit house, I know it welcomed you. Thank you, thank you, thank you. Namaste. The divine in me salutes the divine in you and thanks you for integrating your consciousness with his. He is still there, don't you think? Didn't you feel it? I do. Did you see the wolf? He was Floyd's best friend. I keep wishing the wolf would communicate with me. And sometimes I've gone out there at night and heard a woman trying to tell me something."

"A big-hair woman?"

"I don't know, but she's telling me to make my peace with the world and that's what I'm trying to do. Come over, Jimmy. I need to see you." So he zipped up his parka and, though he hadn't ordered any breakfast, he slipped a twenty-dollar bill under a used coffee cup on the counter. Myrt was watching his reflection in the toaster. She didn't miss a trick. He headed for the door, and she was on the twenty like a bald eagle on a bunny.

15. A séance with Faye

Faye was a fool, but sometimes fools have a good message in among their foolishness, and so James steeled himself with a cup of coffee and marched down to Faye's little house with the wind chimes dinging and tinkling on the front porch and the sign on the front door, ABANDON FEAR AND PREJUDICE, ALL YE WHO ENTER HERE, and knocked on the door. She was right there, waiting for him. "Come in," she cried. "Oh you look exhausted. Oh it is good to see you!" She took some white powder from her pocket and tossed it over his left shoulder and the right and dropped some at his feet and then hugged him. "You and I are kinsmen, Jimmy. We are family. We are interconnected whether we know it or not. We nurture each other with our common myths and rituals, and in each other we find a wholeness of wisdom."

He heard water dripping from a waterfall trickling into a plastic pond with several rather lethargic goldfish. A tea kettle whistled in the kitchen, and she went to make them a pot of tea. Her hair had an ethereal, see-through reddish color.

He noticed when she turned her back that she'd put on weight. She wore a big, white, frilly dress and it was broad in the beam. Interconnected or not, the woman was eating like a horse. On the walls were large color photographs—three feet by four—landscapes: corn stubble, a snowy field, a creek bed with three big cottonwood trees rising from it, an abandoned farm site, another abandoned farm site, and then a full-frontal view of a naked woman of advanced years, in black and white. He didn't want to look at it, but it was hard not to. "That's a self-portrait," she said. He had guessed as much. "It took me forty years to get up the courage to do that," she said. He thought it might've been better if she hadn't waited so long, but he didn't say anything.

"I have so much I want to share with you," she said. A crystal chandelier hung from the ceiling. A low ceiling and an enormous chandelier, so you had to walk around it. She had glued various clay figures to the chandelier: horses and bears, some Indian figures, a couple of coyote. "I bought that in Tucson," she said. "And then when Floyd died, I moved back here because his spirit is here and my work is here." She was storytelling in schools and doing some life coaching and trying to earn extra money by selling Greenspring organic skin cleanser, moisturizer, eyeliner, mascara, and blush, and her sister, Liz, was boycotting her because some of the products were made in Communist China, so she and

Liz were not speaking, but they had often not spoken in the past, so it was no hardship.

"How's your Christmas?" he said.

"Oh Jimmy," she said. "Don't you feel it? Christmas is the force field of heightened possibility. It's not about religion; those myths we were brought up with are only tools to direct us toward the mystery of the under self. It's about the ecstatic visualization of psychic metaphor. The psychic world is calling us toward balanced consciousness. Don't you feel that? There is a lightness and spontaneity that is struggling to get through all the commercial static and lead us out of our linear consciousness into a global wholeness. You know about global wholeness, don't you?"

He nodded. Yes, of course.

"I feel so connected to you right now," she said. He sensed a hug coming on and he edged away.

She collected spoons and cups. Spoons, she explained, represented the generosity of life. So did cups. Hundreds of them hung on hooks on the wall. Wooden spoons, steel spoons, shallow spoons, deep spoons. "This can be good for you spiritually, coming back to Looseleaf. I know you came to see Daddy, but really I think you've come here to find yourself, and I want to help you if I can. I've become a bard, Jimmy. A visionary conversationalist.

"My roots are here. Like yours, Jimmy. And I went away,

as you did, because I felt a polarization between myself and my family. I had to live away until I was ready to come back. And when I was, then I was ready to find the road to spiritual growth in the beautiful motherness of the North Dakota prairie. My consciousness had to evolve from a reliance on mountain wisdom to a trust in prairie wisdom. There are visionary mother spirits here who want to guide us, but we need to be open to dialogue and the goal of transforming consciousness and opening the winter veil to evolutionary experience that nurtures the diversity of the heart that can make us whole."

She wanted to tell him the story of how she got started telling Ojibway tales, and he got up from the table. "Back in a minute," he said, and headed for the door.

"It's cold out there!"

"I know. Gotta start the car."

"Scooter's going to come and start it."

He pretended not to hear her. He got into the parka and barreled out the door. It was brutally cold. He checked WeatherX on his phone and it said minus thirty-eight. His big boots crunched in the snow like walking on cornflakes. The painful sound of cars being started that only wanted to die. But she was right. He had come here to find himself. The bears were in their dens, the honeybees in their hives, the rabbits were browsing in the snow along with the squirrels, their hieroglyphic tracks were everywhere, and he belonged here as much as any of them.

Forty-two years ago, in Fargo, his mother was nine months, two weeks, and ten minutes pregnant, and his jittery father thought she should head for the hospital just in case, since the radio was talking about a blizzard, but she said no, she wanted to watch *The DuPont Christmas Cavalcade* with Milton Berle, Fred Waring and His Pennsylvanians, and *Kukla, Fran and Ollie* on their old Muntz TV, and besides, the hospital was only thirteen blocks away. So she got herself comfy on the couch with a big bowl of buttered popcorn and a gallon of Dad's root beer. When the blizzard rolled in, Daddy got in a royal panic, charging to and fro and hollering about how nobody ever listened to him around here, and that brought on the labor pains. He walked her to the car and a wave of pain hit her and she screamed, which unnerved Daddy so that he drove the wrong way through the blizzard, and thirty-seven miles later, realizing his error, he made a U-turn right into a ditch. He ripped off his car door and lay Mother on it and slid her through the storm to a farmhouse, where James Monroe Sparrow arrived, delivered by an old farmwoman with a basin of hot water and some clean rags shouting at Mother in Polish to squat over the clean towel and push. Meanwhile, the farmwoman went out and strangled a chicken with her two knobby hands and made chicken soup. Mother groaned and tiny James wailed, the midwife cut the umbilicus with a paring knife and taped it with duct tape, and then she looked around for Daddy. He had gone to the cellar to get away from the yelling and gotten into the slivovitz and now, three sheets to the wind, he was on his way to shovel out the car, wearing only a white shirt and trousers. She clubbed him with a rolling pin and barricaded him in a closet and likely saved his life. The story was in the news and they were too embarrassed to go back to Fargo, so they went to Mother's hometown of Looseleaf and Daddy got a job with Uncle Earl at the power plant. He was the bookkeeper.

Winter made James feel like a child. Trapped. In Looseleaf, winter came hard and fast; in a few days the world turned brown and gray and the house creaked as it shrank.

Snow fell, then more and more. And more. The lake froze over and it sounded like gunfire, the ice hardening. Blizzards blew down from Canada and came in suddenly and unexpectedly.

There was no weather forecasting, just a strong sense of foreboding—old Great-Aunt Cooter sitting by the wood stove, an old snaggletoothed crone wrapped in tattered quilts, grizzled, rheumy-eyed, gumming her food, tobacco juice dripping down her chin, listening to the wind in the chimney, and she'd hoist herself up and roll her blue-gray eyes and croak like a tree toad, *It's a gonna be a bad one, chillun.* That was the forecast. And it always was a bad one.

The town lay on flat open prairie, no windbreaks, just barbed wire, and the sky turned a metallic gray and got very low overhead and two or three feet of snow fell for a day or two and the wind blew it horizontally so that you could not see your hand in front of your face. And then the temperature dropped. To the manly men of North Dakota, winter was a challenge. Zero was considered a mild chill. Twenty below was cold. Forty below was darned cold. At sixty below you had to take precautions. They'd bundle up and go out to start the car, which would be frozen solid in the driveway. They'd put on great mackinaws and four-buckle overshoes and caps with earflaps, and out into the storm they'd go, and when they raised the hood it would screech so loud the icicles fell off the house, huge forty-five-pounders like giant daggers of ice crashing and splintering.

The teenaged James hid in a little nest in a crawl space up over the kitchen. It was warm in there, and he ran an extension cord to plug a lamp in and he lay on old car cushions under army blankets and read books from the library, pounds of them, books about Africa and India and the Amazon, and sailing on a tramp steamer to New Guinea, and about czarist Russia and the Count and Countess Ouspenskaya in their palace and the lovely Ludmilla with her high cheekbones and Prince Sergei with the flashing blue eyes awaiting the revolutionaries, who will attack in the morning and interrupt their beautiful romance. But tonight Ludmilla, in her diaphanous white gown, is playing Chopin in the drawing room for the young man in the cavalry uniform, whose blue cigar smoke drifts through the candlelight, and he steps out onto the terrace, and snow is falling all across Russia, and the delicious summer and fall have ended and now the grim winter of terror and desolation has begun, and outside he could hear Daddy calling his name, angry, demanding that he come downstairs immediately and start shoveling and help start the car.

And now here he was, thirty years later and two blocks away, feeling pretty good despite wind chill of minus eighty.

He got in Faye's old Buick and it started right up and her radio came on. Public radio. A psychologist talking about feelings of alienation experienced during cold snaps and how people can combat this by dressing warmly. While the engine ran, James swept the walk, and then stood, the sting of cold air in his nose, and felt exhilarated. Especially when he spotted the old pumps in the yard next door. The man collected antiques and he had six pumps, their handles at five o'clock, waiting for someone doomed by fate to put a tongue on them, but James was no longer that man. He was free. He went back into the house.

"I met the wolf and he's Ralph, my old friend who

drowned duck hunting when he was twenty-five. I am hoping to see him again. And I am on a twenty-four-hour pass from the spirit world to make my peace with everyone, and I have no idea what happens after that."

Faye hugged him. She held him close. Nothing she said had ever made much sense to him and yet there was a fundamental goodness in her that appealed to him, much as he had always made fun of it in the past. She was a good woman in her own fogbound way. "I love you, Faye," he said. She thought about that for a long moment, perhaps waiting for him to say more, maybe something about global wholeness. Then she said, "I love you, James."

Good to know. Good to get that out there.

16. He meets his dying uncle who is in fine fettle indeed

He left Faye's and passed Uncle Boo's house and remembered the smell of peppermint schnapps, and across the street was Uncle Sherm's, who sat on that porch night after night, stone-faced, smelling of mothballs, his hair matted, and all he said was "Is that so?" and "How 'bout that?"

Second Coming was this morning, Uncle Sherm. *Is that so?* Jesus came and took all the believers to heaven for an eternity of bliss. *How 'bout that.* Everyone in the family except you and me, Uncle Sherm. *Is that so?* But meanwhile we can drive their cars and eat all their frozen steaks. *How 'bout that.*

Through the falling snow, he saw Uncle Earl's little red-roofed bungalow nestled in big drifts with narrow canyons where the walks had been shoveled. Heavy plastic was nailed over the storm windows for extra insulation. A few lights were on inside, and on the front porch was a jumble of electrical cables and fuse boxes and generators. Earl liked to keep his hand in. James opened the front door and a wave of warmth rolled out and the smell of baked chicken. But not ordinary chicken. This had special spices in it. The living room seemed more orderly than he remembered. The antimacassar on top of the old upright piano was spotless, and the busts of Schumann, Chopin, Bach, and Mozart had been shined up.

The red throw on the old green sofa was straight, the copies of *North Dakota Geographic* were neatly stacked, the fish tank bubbled away, the goldfish maneuvered through the plastic vegetation, and the carpet where Uncle Earl liked to strew his books was clear—the books were lined up on the bookcase, a sure sign that the occupant of the house was no longer in charge.

Aunt Myrna's collection of china birds had been dusted. From the kitchen came a wave of wonderful chicken aroma. Someone—he guessed it might be Oscar's wife—had opened the oven door and squirted butter on it. He called out, "Hello?" and a dark woman's face peered around the corner. She was short and fat and wrapped in red silk and wore large thin loops of gold around her neck. Her black hair was tied into two braids with a silver thread braided into it. Silvery shapes of sheep and goats were woven into the red silk wrap. She wore gilded sandals.

"I'm James Sparrow. I'm Uncle Earl's nephew from Minneapolis."

She bowed. "My name is Rosana," she said. "I am his caregiver. He is all excited about you coming. He's in the toilet now."

The kitchen had been scrubbed and polished way beyond the norm. The wood floor shone, and two red rugs had been laid down by the breakfast nook. For years the nook had been a holding area for stuff in transition, but now it was back in business again. Two thin blue tapers in silver holders, two red woven placemats—it was as if Uncle Earl had found a new wife.

Rosana was of indeterminate age. Indian, apparently. She was doing a fine job of making a martini, chipping the ice cubes, chilling the glass in the freezer, as she said, "Oh my, yes. I have heard very much good about you. All of it good. A very, very good man. Oh yes. He talks of you many, many times. Goodness, yes. And also of your lovely wife. How very, very lucky for us that you could take time from your busy life and come visit us, Mr. Sparrow.

"But I talk too much. Here I am zipping my mouth with the zipper of silence and I am locking it shut and now I am putting the key in my pocket until you tell me to talk."

"Okay. Thank you."

"Please converse with your dear uncle, Mr. Sparrow, knowing that you shall have the silence you require. I am being still now."

"Thank you."

"Rosana will be quiet until you tell me to talk. Then I will talk. But now I am quiet. I will observe your wishes in the matter. And would you also wish a martini?"

It was 10:00 a.m. Early for a martini. But why not? "Of course."

So she chilled a second glass and chipped more ice, and then there was a rustle and a low chuckle and Uncle Earl appeared, in blue bathrobe, pajamas, and slippers, thinner and paler but moving forward on his own power. A bad case of bed hair, but the moustache was trim and the pajamas were clean. James stepped up and put his arms around him. He had shrunk somehow; the towering figure of James's youth had become dwarflike, but he still twinkled like the good old uncle of old. And he was carrying a plastic bag with a tube that seemed to be stuck in his abdomen.

"So you met my new girlfriend, then?"

"You're a lucky man, Uncle Earl. She's taking good care of you."

"Eighty-six and I'm still attractive to the ladies, James."

Rosana poured the gin into the shaker and a dash of vermouth and put the cap on and shook it, and Uncle Earl twitched his hips in a sort of mambo. The plastic bag in his hand made a squoshy sound.

"I heard you were at death's door, Uncle Earl."

"They were all set to put me in the ground, James. They bought the charcoal briquettes to make the fire to heat up the ground so they could dig the grave. The coffin was on order from Grand Forks. The doctor had his death certificate all filled out, month and year, everything except for the date and time. And then the county welfare office told us we were eligible for home hospice care, and Liz was telling them no, and I raised my head up off the pillow and said I wanted to die at home, and so they sent Rosana. A miracle worker. She got here and drove the death squad out and made me a martini and I've been in tall clover ever since."

"It is as God wills it to be," she said, ducking her head modestly, smiling, and she poured the liquor into the two glasses and put them on a tray with a dish of chips and a greenish dip and led the way into the living room.

"I always meant to take you places, Uncle Earl. Soon as this storm blows over, we could fly you out to Hawaii. I know about a wonderful place out there."

"I saw Hawaii when I was in the service. Honolulu. Gyp joints and dance halls and girls hanging on you begging you to dance with them and buy them a fifty-dollar bottle of five-dollar champagne. No need to go back and see it again."

"Or we could fly you to the Mayo Clinic and see if they can't address some of your health issues."

"I'm eighty-six years old. I used up my time. But I made up my mind I want to go out with a big party. And here you are. So we're going to put away the black crepe and have us a big Christmas. And maybe a New Year's. And then I'm ready to go."

The old man followed Rosana into the living room and sat down in his big green armchair, and she spread a comforter on his lap and turned an electric heater on his feet and lit a couple of candles and handed him his martini.

"What's in the plastic bag, Uncle Earl?"

"What? This?" The old man looked down at the bag in his hand as if he'd forgotten all about it. "It's my liver and pancreas, James. They were going to do a transplant, but they discovered, after they got it out, that the other liver wasn't the right shape, so they're waiting for another donor, and meanwhile, got my liver here in the bag, along with the pancreas, and they're working okay. Not great, but okay."

James was going to say something about Mayo doing great work in transplants, but decided not to. He looked out the window at the Christmas lights on the rambler across the street, a thousand of them burning bright through the night.

"That's the Guntzels. When he turns them all on at night, I get phone conversations on my radio. I was listening to one when you came in. Man telling his mother why his family couldn't come for Christmas this year, and it was all a tissue of lies about these other things they had to do. Ha. They couldn't come because they didn't want to come, was the truth of the matter, and the old lady kept trying to fix it so they could. It was sad."

James sat down and smelled the gin. "I just saw Faye. She looks pretty good."

"That's her art on the wall." James looked over at a canvas with white drips spackled onto it, entitled *Beginnings, Endings, Connections, Continuations*.

"She doesn't earn much money from her art, but she enjoys it."

"And Oscar?"

"We don't see much of him in the winter months. He just sort of slows down, and he wasn't going fast to begin with."

"And Liz?"

"Busy saving the country from totalitarianism, last I heard. Where you staying, by the way? I'd have you stay here, James, but Rosana's got the guest room."

"It's okay. I've got a place to stay."

They sat in silence for a while and the old man's eyes closed. James thought, *What if he croaks right now?* The old man's chest seemed to be moving, but he couldn't tell. *At what point should I go over and listen for a heartbeat?* And then Uncle Earl smiled and said:

"I had a Swedish grandpa who went crazy here one winter. It was before there were snowplows, and he stayed out on his farm for five months straight because he believed there was gold on his land and he didn't want anybody to steal it. There wasn't any, and we never could figure out how he came to think there was, but he was convinced he was sitting on fields of gold. Maybe he read it in a book. His kids he had boarded with families in town so they could attend school, and his wife stayed there to see to them, and he was snowbound on the farm week after week through one blizzard after another, living in the kitchen and burning as little wood as he needed to stay alive, feeding the livestock, nobody to talk to, and when they found him in the spring, he was extremely uncommunicative and there was madness in his pale blue eyes. He got himself cleaned up and went to church and plowed his fields, but he was mad, and when summer rolled around he got to drinking fermented blackstrap molasses and stayed out late howling at the moon and came home with blood and feathers around his mouth. They sent him to the state hospital in Jamestown and put him in leg irons, and my mother wouldn't let us go visit him, but I snuck away, I felt it was my duty, and I found him in a little room, chained to his bed, and he was happy in his own mind, he was living in a castle in Fargo with forty-three servants to wait on him and he was going to spend the winter in Hawaii. He had a pineapple ranch there. It was all clear in his own mind. The state hospital didn't exist for him. That room with the peeling plaster walls he considered to be a complete fiction. He was going to Hawaii."

It was a good martini.

"There was a lot of insanity going around. I remember the faith healer who came to warm us up one winter. From Texas. Waco, Texas. Presbyterian. All a matter of faith, he said. He was a thin man with deep-set eyes, wore a seersucker suit and a straw hat, carried his stuff in a cardboard suitcase, walked into various people's homes and cried out in tongues and tied fishline to their wrists and sprinkled sparkle dust around them, and around Halloween it got down into the fifties, too cold for him, and he was shivering so bad, he couldn't wash nor shave nor button a button, and he lay there under a mountain of quilts and pleaded with us to give him money for a train ticket home, and we held out until the middle of November and we got tired of having to bring him his meals in bed and we sprang for a one-way ticket to Dallas. We had to drive him to Bismarck to catch the train and we had to put a fat girl on either side of him to keep him warm. And he lost his faith then and there. North Dakota winter made him question the existence of a loving God. He went back to Texas and learned to shuffle a deck of cards so as to put the cards he needed in a place where he could find them. He earned his living playing Texas-draw poker in the back rooms of pool halls and he had beautiful women to keep him warm, and the last we heard, he'd been elected to Congress."

Uncle Earl sat and beamed at him and sipped his gin. "It's good to have you here."

"Sorry I haven't been back to visit you. I meant to." James stared at the plastic bag, wondering what a liver and pancreas looked like. Did he dare ask for a peek?

Uncle Earl waved away the apology like a mosquito. "It's okay." He beamed some more. For a man who was about to dive underground, he was in a highly jovial mood. "You were a good kid, James. Your mother and dad worried so much about you they never got to enjoy you, but I did. And now look at you. You're young and in your prime and ready to conquer the world."

"Just trying to conquer myself, Uncle Earl."

Uncle Earl thought about this for a moment. "I could've done more with my life, but I've got no regrets. I had a nice job offer in Minneapolis once. More money, an office, carpeted, with a view of Loring Park. But the guy who made me the offer had this smirky look on his face like he'd done me the biggest favor and he expected me to kiss his tasseled loafer—Minneapolis! He was offering me Minneapolis! I looked him in the eye and said, 'No thanks, I'd rather stay where I am. Looseleaf, North Dakota. Good people.' Which was true. Leeds Cutter. There was a classy man. Practiced law here. Before your time. Had an office up over the bank. Sat up there and read books and sketched in his notepad and talked about everything except the law, talked about the Milky Way, the Civil War, bird migration, Duke Ellington, the secret of raising corn and soybeans, the breeding of cattle. Everything interested him. I never saw him in a sour mood. He and Al and Deloyd and Charlie—we were all best friends. Started the Halloween parade back in 1938, you know. Every time I saw those guys, it made me happy. No matter what else was going on, we always sat down and shot the bull and had some laughs. Never too busy to stop and talk. I tell you, that is a rare thing these days. So I have no regrets. You can't put a price on friendship, I say. No man is a failure who has friends."

"So what's your big hurry to leave?"

"It is what it is. This'll be my last Christmas. I can feel it. I'm on my way out, just like that African violet. A race to the finish. My mother took a long time dying. She'd get close and we'd all gather around her bed, and the old worry instinct kicked in and she started asking if we'd had supper and did we have colds and were we getting enough sleep, and pretty soon she'd forgotten about dying and the next day she had to start all over. It's not recommended."

The old man was starting to nod now and Rosana was in the doorway, smiling, waiting to escort Uncle Earl to his nap. It was past noon. James stood up to go, though he didn't know where he was going. "See you tomorrow," he said.

"Good-bye. God bless you," said Rosana. Uncle Earl was dozing already.

"Want me to help get him to bed?"

"I'll get him there. I do it every day."

He touched the old man's forehead. "Thank you for everything," he whispered. Rosana reached down and picked up the bag with the liver and pancreas and put her other hand under Earl's left armpit. "Come on, old man," she said. "Come to bed, darling. Come, my love."

17. Leo's secret mission

James put the crusty old parka back on and a pair of insulated boots and lumbered out the back door and down the alley. The Methodist Men's Christmas tree lot had balsam firs and Scotch pine and spruce, and a sign said CLOSED PAY WHAT U CAN, so he took a little spruce and stuck a hundred-dollar bill in the slot and put it over his shoulder. He stopped at Swedlund's Grocery and bought a bag of strong licorice, a package of Swedish meatballs, a bottle of chili sauce, a box of crackers. He didn't recognize the lady at the cash register. She said, "You're lucky, we close at noon." He was delaying going back to Floyd's shack for fear of what he might find there—open the door and walk into what? A concert hall where he'd have to sing his aria from *Messiah*? A hockey arena and he'd be the goalie on the losing side? He stepped into Phil's Happy Hour for a bottle of cognac. The bartender was tall with loose skin, like he'd just lost a hundred pounds or so. It was barely noon and men sat at the bar drinking their beer with shots of whiskey and watching an electric Santa in dark glasses play a guitar and sing "I Yust

Go Nuts at Christmas," and none of them seemed amused, though his belly shook like a bowlful of jelly and his guitar burst into flames. An old woman sat in a booth, a bottle of beer in front of her, three empty ones, and yelled into her cell phone: "You do exactly what you want to do because that's what you're going to do anyway, so there's no point in my arguing with you. I don't want anybody coming to my house for Christmas because they feel they have an obligation to. I would frankly rather spend Christmas alone with a frozen turkey dinner than be with people who don't enjoy my company."

The person at the other end tried to get in a word, and she said, "No, no—that's fine—you made your choice, now stick with it. And merry Christmas." She snapped the cell phone shut and set it down on the table. It rang, and she ignored it. The bartender searched under the bar and came up with a bottle of Armagnac. "Kinda steep," he said. "Forty bucks."

James gave him sixty. "That's for you. Merry Christmas."

The temperature had dropped to forty below zero. He noticed that minus forty was as low as any thermometer in Looseleaf went—the little one attached to Earl's kitchen window, the big one beside the front door of the Westendorp Pure Oil station, and the Cobb's Super Foods thermometer—evidently forty below zero was as much cold as anyone here cared to know about. But he was toasty warm in the big boots and balloon parka that had belonged to the late Floyd. He trudged along the path toward the lake and out onto the ice and got to Floyd's just as a snowmobile came buzzing alongside, and stopped, idling and sputtering, and it was Leo Wimmer.

"Hey," he said. "I looked for you at Earl's and they said you'd come out here. Mind if I come in and sit for a while?" He stepped into Floyd's shack before he could be disinvited, and took off his coat and sat down, and James poured a couple fingers of Armagnac into a Dixie cup. And one finger into a second cup for himself. For mouthwash.

Leo was hot to talk: "Man's got to live his own life and not somebody else's. That's the dilemma. Floyd got trapped into Arizona. Tucson was Faye's idea, not his. He had nothing to do with it. She was gone most of the time, running around doing her Ojibway thing, talking up duality and global consciousness and so forth, and Floyd was left to wash the windows and water the lawn. But every January he managed to escape up here for a few weeks and sit in his fish house and enjoy the good life. He loved this old shack. He told me it was just like going to church, except you didn't have to shake hands with people you don't like."

Leo took a seat by the fish hole and looked at the bobber in the water. "Liz is always after me to devote myself to the cause, but it isn't exactly my cause. That's the whole problem with marriage. Trying to maintain your true course in life and not get sucked into the gravitational field of the spouse.

She says to me, 'Why don't you ever want to go to meetings with me?' She loves meetings. The Possum Comatosis. The Oak Tree Society. The Citizens for Life. You name it, she goes. Loves to go to town meetings organized by Democrats and yell and wave signs. That's her. But it isn't me."

"I guess I always assumed you were more or less in her camp," James said. "I mean, you two are both National Rifle Association—you met at a gun show, right?"

Leo nodded. "I never told anybody this, but I feel like I can trust you, James. I was there at the gun show working undercover for the FBI. And I still am."

"You're with the FBI?"

Leo closed his eyes. "You're the first person I told this to. It's been a horrible burden."

"Who are you spying on, if I may ask?"

"Liz."

"The FBI has you spying on your wife?"

Leo tossed back a swig of Armagnac. "She is plotting to overthrow the government of the United States. She and a couple hundred others. She's deadly serious."

"And you're sleeping with her?"

"The only way I could get into her life undetected was for her to fall in love with me. So I seduced her. They have pharmaceuticals for that, you know. Hallucinogens. Two drops of it on a pretzel and she was climbing on my lap like a monkey."

"So you went undercover and got under the covers?"

"She's a very nice woman when she isn't all het up about conspiracies. We have a reasonably good marriage. Except I know that one day I will have to snap the cuffs on her and haul her in for trying to bring down the government."

"How exactly is she planning to do that?"

"Internet hacking. She's got sixteen guys working out of a basement room in the power plant. Your uncle's retired but he still runs the electric co-op, and Liz has established a super-high-speed accelerated Internet center there that specializes in hacking into bank accounts and moving large sums of money around."

James looked at the little man in the big parka and wondered if a fairy tale was being spun here before his eyes. But the little man reached into his parka and opened up a Velcro pocket halfway down the left sleeve and pulled out a badge. Federal Bureau of Investigation. Special Agent.

"Not that you ever would," he said, "but there's a hefty penalty for exposing the identity of an undercover agent."

And then the ice boomed, and Leo winced and got to his feet. "I'll fill you in on the rest later," he said, and exited, and the snowmobile engine revved and it buzzed away. It sounded like the cardboard James and Ralph used to fasten to their bike fenders to flap against the spokes and make a sort of engine sound. One summer they rode in and around

Looseleaf with flaps buzzing and out the western road to the marsh and laid their bikes down in the tall grass and stripped and went in swimming, the skinny dark James, the skinny blond Ralph. There was a crystal-clear pool with lush lily pads in an inlet under overhanging cottonwoods and they lay around in there and thought out loud about various things—

Planes overhead: where are they going?

Do your parents have sex?

When will we die and what will happen then?

If you could be anyone in the world right now, who would it be?

What if a meteor hits the Earth and knocks it off orbit so that North Dakota becomes the tropics and the Caribbean is the new North Pole?

What if God told you to kill somebody, would you do it?

What if you had a million dollars?

The two of them were mostly agreed on basic principles: the planes were headed for California, carrying criminals and movie stars; parents did not have sex anymore—they had tried it once or twice and it didn't interest them; we will die when we are extremely old, like in our fifties; we would be either Clint Eastwood or Steve Cannon; if North Dakota became the tropics, it would be horrible and everyone would have to move away, perhaps to Mexico; you would kill that person, but only if you were 100 percent sure; you would take your million dollars and put it in the bank at 3 percent interest and roam the world, Asia and South America, stay in ritzy hotels, eat steaks and ice cream, have a heckuva time.

It was from the shore near the pool by the cottonwoods that Ralph launched the canoe to go retrieve the dead ducks that October afternoon. He was twenty-five years old. Seventeen years ago.

He and James used to skate on their long blades at this end of the lake, side by side, hands behind their backs, watchful of the spot off the end of the point where a spring bubbles up and the ice can be soft. People had gone through the ice there and in very cold weather that would be the end of you, but they were two skating together, so the other one would help the guy out of the slush and get him to shelter.

And Ralph saved his life that time on the camping trip out in the muskeg, north of there, when Elmer took Troop 147 camping on the coldest night in January, though some parents said, "What if one of the boys wanders away? He could die of exposure." Elmer said, "That will teach them to stick close together." Around the campfire Elmer told a story about a Scoutmaster who rescued a boy from a freezing lake and saved him from hypothermia by stripping off his clothes and lying naked in a sleeping bag with him, warming him with the heat of his own body, which seemed extremely weird to the boys, and all night long they kept one eye open for him.

Memories of that night. How, having walked out in the snow to pee, James wrote in the snow, "Theresa, I love you," and how, when he was lost, he saw a steel pole sticking up out of the snow. A surveyor's rod. And a voice in his head said, *You are going to walk over and put your tongue on it and there is absolutely nothing you can do to prevent this.*

He cried at the thought of his imminent death. The tears froze on his cheeks. The voice said, *Why wait? Why postpone the inevitable? Put your tongue on the rod. You know in your heart you will do it. Do it now.* He thought of his weeping mother following the pine box carried over the frozen ground by six townsmen in heavy parkas and his own body riding inside, in the cheap satin plush, and the preacher hurrying the prayer of commitment, his teeth chattering, and then the coffin falling slowly down into the depths of the frozen earth, and then a hand touched his shoulder and he jumped six feet and turned, and it was Ralph. "You better come back," he said. James followed him up the ravine. "Why did you write my girlfriend's name in the snow?" Ralph said. "That's a different Theresa," said James, lying. "You don't know her. She's not from here." "That better be the truth," said Ralph.

And now Ralph had returned in the form of a gray wolf to give James the benefit of his insight, and his cousin-in-law Leo was an FBI agent about to arrest Liz and break the heart of Uncle Earl, who was walking around with his liver and pancreas in a plastic bag. Amazing facts, but then, the world is full of them.

18. In the Coyote Coffee Shop on Parnassus Avenue, he meets his wise man

He stepped out on the ice and walked around back of the shack to take a leak and for the nth time was stunned by the beauty of the fresh snow, the frozen lake shining, cold and beautiful. And thought of his own death. He had come into the world around Christmastime, and maybe he'd be leaving it too, to satisfy nature's craving for symmetry. The world would exist without him in it. The Coyote Corp. would go on and Billy Jack Morosco wouldn't even notice his absence and Mrs. Sparrow would grieve and then move on and meet Larry and not much would change.

And then a light tap-tap-tap-tap on the door. Someone inside Floyd's shack, inviting him in. A strange sound. People around here knock three times—*knock knock knock*. Or some people knock five—*knock knock knock knock knock*.

This was four: *taptaptaptap*.

He zipped up and kicked clean snow on top of the yellow snow and walked around the shack and opened the door and walked into a coffee shop where a young man with a prominent beak and big eyebrows and a shaved head stood at the counter, the espresso machines behind him, and a cap on his head that said COYOTE COFFEE. The room was full of customers perusing newspapers or tapping away at laptops, young women in black, young men in billboard T-shirts, not a parka or pair of mittens in sight. An Asian man stood looking at the pastries; he wore a shirt with the Golden Gate bridge painted on the back. He smelled of a rich fragrance James had never encountered before.

The man behind the counter said, "May I help you?" and James said, "Where am I?"

The man didn't blink. He said, "Parnassus Street. The Inner Sunset. San Francisco."

"Aha. Then I'll have a large latte with an extra shot. And a biscotti."

"For here or to go?"

"For here." Why would a person buy a latte on Parnassus Street in San Francisco and take it out onto a frozen lake in North Dakota?

He knew without looking that he would not have money in his pocket. *Of course* he would not have money in his pocket—that is in the nature of fables. The pocket is empty. Money buys you nothing here. All is fate and magic. And when the latte was made and the tall cup and the biscotti set down on the counter and he had explained to the coffee man that he was extremely sorry but he had no money on him, he had left home without it, the man grinned and said, "You're very funny, Mr. Sparrow. This is a story. Coffee's on the house."

He carried his coffee to the one empty seat in the café, at a table in the window, where an old Chinese man sat dozing over his newspaper.

"Is this seat taken?" The Chinese man opened his eyes and gestured for him to sit down.

Outdoors, a trolley swung around the corner screeching and a woman pushed a stroller past with four sleeping babies in it, a full load.

"Pardon me," said Mr. Sparrow, "but I don't have much time. Twenty-four hours, in fact, and it's almost up, and this being a fable—and I think I know how fables work—you're supposed to speak some sort of wisdom to me. I mean, it's pretty obvious—one seat open in the whole café—and so maybe we could get right to it and if there's something more I need to do to win a reprieve, then I'll have time to do it. Okay?"

The old Chinese man looked at him and blinked. "Sparrow?" he said.

"Sparrow."

The Chinese man reached into his pocket for a looseleaf

notebook and paged through it slowly, looking at each sheet on which he had written dense lines of script in a fountain-pen hand. "Is this about sins of the flesh? Nevada?"

"No, no, no—I'm from Minneapolis. I'm the guy who used to not like Christmas and then I was given twenty-four hours to get straightened out and my cousin Liz chopped a hole in the ice and I jumped in and it sort of unblocked things for me—anyway, the name is Sparrow. S-p-a-r-r-o-w."

"Oh. *Sparrow.* Yes. Mr. Sparrow."

The old Chinese man peered at him closely and poured hot water into a tea cup and then flinched—he'd spilled some on his leg. James wasn't sure that a wise man in a fable should be doing that sort of thing, but he waited.

"This morning I saw a sparrow in a tree, a variety of sparrow I've never seen before. A blue-billed one. He looked at me with a cocked eye and I waited and waited and finally he flew up and dropped a slip of paper at my feet, a message meant for you. It says, 'Today you will be very lucky with the number three if you wait at the trolley stop where the lady with the red parasol spoke to you about your brother Frank.'"

"I have no brother Frank. My name is Sparrow. James Sparrow."

The man dropped a teabag in the hot water. "James Sparrow?" James nodded.

"Ah yes. Very good. Very, very good." The old Chinese man closed his eyes again and leaned his head back against the wall and seemed to snooze for a minute and James was about to nudge his foot and then the old man said softly, "I am in touch with the one who rules your fate, whatever you wish to call her."

James felt his heart clench and the room seemed to inhale and contract. He felt a coronary occlusion coming on and in two seconds he'd pitch forward onto the floor and lie there, trying to draw breath.

And then his phone rang. He looked at the old man, who nodded. "Answer it," he said. "I have plenty of time."

It was Mrs. Sparrow. "Darling? How are you?" she said.

"I'm fine. Enjoying a heckuva snowstorm."

"How's Uncle Earl?"

"He got himself an attractive Indian caregiver and now he's sitting up and taking nourishment. Listen, sweetheart—"

"Will you make it home for Christmas?"

"Airport's still snowed in, darling. How's your flu? Did you go see the doctor about it?"

"I did, and he gave me the big news. I'm expecting a baby."

The old man smiled at James and pressed his palms together and bowed slightly.

James could not speak.

"I miss you," she said. "I miss you terribly. You're the most giving and generous person I know and now you've given me what I wanted most. Are you there?"

He was there, but he didn't have the power of speech just now.

She said, "I'll call you back—" And then another trolley came rolling by. And then the phone went dead.

The old Chinese man said, "You are a lucky man, Mr. Sparrow. You almost married Theresa Donderewicz, and that would have been a terrible mistake. It was December. You were nineteen years old and desperate to be loved and she seemed willing and you went for a walk at night and wound up in the cemetery and you lied to her about how you planned to go to law school and the truth was, you'd been kicked out of college for extreme nonattendance, but you told her you'd take her to Paris. You didn't know how desperate she was. She went to Fargo and planned to sing and dance and amaze people but found out she wasn't at all amazing in Fargo, only adequate, she learned that Loose-leafers cannot astonish in Fargo, so she cried for three nights, standing under a stoplight, hoping to be discovered by someone special, then went home and saw you. You seemed like a live possibility. So she invited you home and took you into the basement and you two sat on a bed and kissed for a while and took each other's clothes off and were just about to intertwine and then the basement door opened and her father called her name and she answered. You hid in the corner. He came down the stairs and saw her lying under a blanket and she told him she couldn't sleep in her own bed because it was too warm upstairs so she came down there, and then he saw your shoes and your pants. He cursed and went galloping upstairs to get a gun, and you snatched up your clothes and ran out the back way, naked on a bitter cold night, and made it to Uncle Earl's, and he took mercy on you. He told Mr. Donderewicz that you'd been sitting in his kitchen playing pinochle and he described the game in great detail, and Mr. Donderewicz, though suspicious, went snarling away, and your life was saved. Had you done what you intended to do, you'd be driving a truck of liquid nitrogen and enduring your father-in-law's rage and your mother-in-law's alcoholism, and Theresa weighs a good deal more than when you saw her last."

James remembered Theresa. How lonely he was that winter. He'd come home broke and disheartened and worked shoveling sidewalks, and lived in his parents' attic for a month, and every morning Daddy asked him, "When are you going to do something with yourself?" And he didn't know.

"There were numerous occasions when you almost ran off the tracks," said the old man. "I could go down the list if you like. You applied for a job at Radio City Music Hall on that trip to New York when you were twenty-six and so starstruck by New York and the Rockettes and the Christmas show and the tap-dancing Santas. It was a production assistant job and they passed you over for a guy with a BA from Princeton and now he's running a road show of *The Fantasticks* on the junior college circuit and he is rather heavily medicated. And when you met Joyce and she declined the invitation to Mackinac Island, you were disappointed and you invited your old college sweetheart Lolly and she almost said yes. She was free that weekend and was feeling lonely too. I had to intervene that time and give her an oozing cold sore. And then two years after you married Joyce, you took her to New York City to see the shows and you planned to go up to Windows on the World for breakfast and got on the subway, and I had to step in again. In person. Remember the Chinese man who was yelling at you? You and Joyce got off the train at Fourteenth Street to get away from him, and then no more trains came because the two airliners had struck the World Trade Center towers and the restaurant where you'd have been eating your scrambled eggs was full of smoke and soon to fall to the ground. They all died, your fellow diners, and the waiters and the busboys who cleaned the tables."

James had forgotten that, and now it came back: that sunny September morning in New York and the shouting man and the long wait on the Fourteenth Street subway platform, and then they climbed the stairs to the street and people stood on the sidewalk looking downtown at the clouds of black smoke in the sky.

"Why did you save us and not the others?" said James.

"I wasn't told why. I guess it was for your children's sake. Maybe you're producing a Mozart or a Rossini. A Mark Twain. A Rod Carew."

"And what about the others' children?"

"They are held in perpetual light and everlasting blessedness."

The old man leaned across the table. "You are the bene-factor of great blessing. And you have no idea how much goodness is lavished on the world by invisible hands. Small selfless deeds engender tremendous force against the darker powers. Great kindness pervades this world, struggling against pernicious selfishness and vulgar narcissism and the vicious streak that is smeared in each human heart—great bounding goodness is rampant and none of it is wasted. No, these small gifts of goodness—this is what saves the soul of man from despair, and that is what preserves humanity from the long fall from the precipice into the abyss."

So his dream—his habitual nightmare of being hunted in tall grass and attempting to escape and only edging closer to the precipice overlooking the dark abyss, the sharks, the big black birds, etc.

"Yes," said the old Chinese man. "This is not a prophetic dream. It is a revelation of how you have been brought safely over dangerous shoals and through narrow passages unawares. And now your trip to Looseleaf has resulted in much good. You have cheered up your uncle, who was descending toward death and is now having a last encore of pleasure before he leaves."

"When will he die?" said James.

"Tuesday. And you made peace with your cousin, whom you dislike, and you fought your other cousin to a draw, and that was good for her soul, to be withstood. She's had it all her way for most of her life and now there's a little hole in her roof and she can view the sky. Any way you can offer a fellow being a new prospect is a kindness.

"Even your twenty-dollar tip for Myrt, who was embarrassed by the generosity and meant to run after you and give it back, but the truth is, she is short on cash and there is nothing shameful about need nor about what satisfies it. We give and we take. She takes your money which she needs to buy a Frank Sinatra CD, *Songs for Lovers*, and a pack of Camels, and a bottle of beer for her old aunt Lois, who needs to feel twenty-six again and dancing at the Spanish Gardens ballroom in Santa Barbara with Jack McCloskey the textile salesman and her first true love the night they necked in his pink convertible with the night breeze rich with eucalyptus and palm and though she knew he was not long for her arms, still he was gentle and sweet to her and told her he loved her over and over as he made love to her, which, at twenty-six, she had never tasted before, and so this was a revelation that, despite the sarcasm of her sisters and the harsh remarks of her mother, Lois could be loved, and now, years later, listening to Mr. Sinatra and smoking a cigarette in her upstairs bedroom, she will call up Jack, who is seventy-eight years old and languishing in a care center in Provo, Utah, which Myrt located via the Internet, and Aunt Lois will tell Jack McCloskey that the memory of that January night remains a lamp in her heart, and this kind word, after years of sodden despair, will illuminate his night and move him to finally and absolutely sign over his wealth to the Jeremiah Program for single mothers, and thereby considerable goodness will be achieved."

The old Chinese man smiled for the first time in his monologue. "So, you see what you've done, Mr. Sparrow. More than you know."

"What about Christmas?"

"What about it? It's a nice day. Take a long walk. Sing more and talk less. Try putting ginger in the cranberry. It helps."

19. Christmas Eve arrives

He walked out of Coyote Coffee and onto the ice of Lake Winnesissebigosh, leaving the pastel hills of San Francisco for the monochromatic flatness of North Dakota. It had stopped snowing. He could hear distant snowplows scraping the pavement. Maybe the airport would get cleared today, but he wasn't ready to go. It was noon and he was bone tired and lay down and slept in the fish house for a few hours and awoke in the cold and pulled on his boots and walked toward town. It was perfectly quiet, the countryside covered with snowdrifts, and he could hear everything that was happening, and nothing was happening. No doors slammed, no car started, nobody yelling. He passed the Bon Ton Café, and Myrt waved to him gaily. Rosana let him into Uncle Earl's and shushed him—the old man was napping—and James lay down on the couch and fell asleep to the fish tank bubbler, and then suddenly it was Christmas Eve and everyone was there and the room was full of candles, bayberry, cranberry—"You'd think we were Catholic!" said Liz—and the old man was decked out in red pants and a white shirt with light-up bow-tie and a red clown nose and a red headband with a small spring arm that held a sprig of mistletoe over his old white head. He was holding the bag with his liver and pancreas in a plastic flowerpot that played "In the Mood," a gift from a grandchild. He said, "Boy. Time sure flies, doesn't it? Got this flowerpot in 1997. Seems like only yesterday."

Faye wore a long white gown and sequins in her hair and a crown of holly and electric candles, and served saffron buns and coffee. She had brought a centerpiece made from an egg carton and green garbage bag twists, very glittery, pictures of shepherds and angels and Democrats, FDR and JFK and MLK and BHO. Liz glanced at it without comment. Oscar arrived with a great fury of stamping and shaking snow off his pants and walked in, the prodigal brother who wasn't speaking to anybody, and all was forgiven—Liz hugged him and said the cologne he was wearing smelled more like disinfectant and if he had an infection, she wanted to know about it. "That's the cologne you gave me three years ago, called Christmas Charisma. First time I put some on," he said, and he took a cup of coffee and poured cream and sugar in it and sat on a hassock and told James he was looking like a big-city swell. Rosana appeared with a big red stocking for James with a dozen multicolor pens and Post-its and candy and a giant navel orange.

Faye had bought Christmas gifts for everyone, porcelain

trivets from Peru and hand-knitted tea cozies from Costa Rica. "These are made by peasants who were paid a fair wage for them," she said. Everyone examined their trivet, which had paintings of stick people doing things with animals. Liz had brought copies of a book called *Alien Reptiles*, by Ann Coulter, arguing that life-forms from outer space had taken over Washington.

The gifts were wrapped in a big hurry, you could see that—paper scrunched, tape slapped on, no ribbons, no bows—par for the course in these busy times, but he remembered Joyce and how she believed in beautiful wrapping. What's important is not the cash value of the gift but the loving intention of the giver, and you show this by how the gift—even the $1.69 bottle of Swank cologne—is wrapped. The recipient holds this work of art in his hands and notices how perfectly the ribbon is placed and that the bow is handmade and the paper is precisely folded into thin trapezoids at the ends, no creases, no wrinkles, and the perfection of the package serves to delay the opening of the gift, which prolongs anticipation, which heightens pleasure.

And now Joyce had become a package, an elegant, beautifully put together package, containing the germ of a new life. A child who, Lord have mercy, would grow up nerdy, tomboyish, awkward, as she had, and learn elegance from the inside out, which is the best way. His child. His eyes had been opened by the dive into freezing water and the visit to

San Francisco and he wanted to announce the blessed news, but how to explain that he'd heard it via a Chinese man in a dream?

"What are these little crisp round things?" said Liz, pawing through the appetizers.

"Fried pig brains," said Oscar. "They're good. Try one."

"I requested them," said Uncle Earl. "The condemned man gets to choose. I've loved pig brains since I was just a little squirt."

And just then, Leo, who never did this sort of thing, spread his arms and sang, "Hail, hail the gang's all here" in his quavery tenor and flung a handful of sparkle dust over them. He gave James a big hug and whispered, "Don't rat on me. I've got a gun concealed on my person, and if you say one word I'll blow you away, and Earl will have to watch you as you croak, so think about that."

James tried to brush him away. "Get away from me, Judas."

"Oh don't be so dramatic," hissed Leo. "I took an oath to defend my country and I'm going to do it."

"It's Christmas, for mercy's sake."

Leo smirked. "A G-man knows what day it is. I'll promise you this—you keep your mitts off and I'll bust Liz after Earl goes to bed."

Oscar was in the midst of a story—he said, "I remember the time that busload of psychoanalysts got stranded here in

December. What year was that? They were going to a convention in Vancouver and took the bus because they were
afraid to fly. It was a snowy night and the bus rolled into
town and stopped to use the men's room at the Bon Ton
and that took a couple hours because there was just one stall
and they all had to do number two and each of them had his
little ceremonies and reading material and so forth, and by
the time they were done, the roads were drifted over and we
had to put them up for the night. Actually, for three days.
Forty-five short bald men with beards. I remember they
loved macaroni noodles in mushroom soup sauce and
canned tuna and peas. We took them ice fishing, and they
loved that. It was a great novelty to them, sitting in a dark
house and looking at a hole in the ice with a fishline hanging
down and a bobber floating in the water. They sat for hours
watching the bobber, writing in their little notebooks. They
were sad to leave, I remember. Got on the bus and put their
faces to the windows and waved their hankies and away
they went."

"That was in fifty-eight," said Uncle Earl. "I remember.
It was the year I went to Rapid City for the Rural Electrifica-
tion convention."

"Nope. Eighty-five," said Oscar. "I remember it because
eighty-five was when Sandy ran away with Norm, the ag
extension agent."

"She didn't exactly run away," said Liz. "She only went as far as Fargo."

"She went far enough," said Oscar, "but anyway, that's all water under the bridge. Eighty-five. That was a hard winter. We had to eat the cat that year. You ever eat cat? They are not as meaty as they look. It was like pork, except tough. I don't think it's anything that is going to catch on, if you know what I mean. That winter we had to bust up the dining room table for firewood, and you know something? Mahogany does not burn well. Mostly it just smoldered. We got a bad case of head lice that winter, and Aunt Cooter went berserk. Remember that? She was running from room to room, crying out about seeing Jesus up on high and trying to take her clothes off—she was yelling, 'I want to put on the new raiment! Put away this old raiment, put on the new raiment!' Boy, that got tiresome real fast. We kept wrapping her up in sheets and she kept ripping them off. She'd been weak and puny for years, but suddenly she had strength in her arms. It happens when people go berserk. I read that somewhere. We just plain ran out of patience. We threatened to put her in the loony bin, but she was seeing Jesus, so it didn't matter to her. Finally we had to give her a tranquilizer, and I guess we overtranquilized her, because she died. But she went quietly in her sleep, which was how she always wanted to go. And she saw Jesus, so that must have been a comfort. It was too cold to bury her right away, the ground was frozen so hard. They were going to use dynamite, but the families of other dead people objected to that, so we just put her in the tool shed until spring. Stood her up and leaned her against the lumber pile."

"I was in Arizona that winter," said Faye and started to launch into a story about the Hopi. James eyeballed Leo at the other end of the table. His legs were crossed and his right foot was pointing at James. Perhaps the concealed weapon was in the toe of his shoe. There appeared to be a small hole there. James walked around the table to the sideboard to pour himself a glass of punch, and Leo turned in his chair, keeping the right foot aimed at James. Oscar went on.

"That was the winter I went out to check my wolf traps and I slipped and fell on a patch of ice in the driveway. I'd plugged in the car to keep it thawed out and it was too cold and the radiator burst and the antifreeze froze. That's how cold it was. Anyway, I fell wrong and broke my leg and the bone poked right out through my pantleg. Luckily it was so cold I couldn't feel a thing. Well, I picked up some ice chunks and tossed them at the kitchen window, and finally Rocky came and saw me. He was eight. I motioned for him to come help me and pointed to the protruding bone, and finally he came out and stood on the back step. I said, 'Honey, I need you to go in the house and call the ambulance. If you don't, Daddy will freeze to death. Okay?'"

"He said, 'Why did you call me Honey? You never called me Honey before.'

"I said, 'I called you Honey because I love you. You're my son and I love you dearly.'

"He said, 'Why didn't you ever say so before?'

"I said, 'Because I didn't want you to get the big head.'

"He said, 'Before I call the ambulance, is it okay if I watch TV for an hour?'

"I said, 'If you do that, Daddy will freeze to death and you'll feel just awful.'

"He said, 'Oh.' And then he asked how much money I'd give him to call the ambulance. I offered him candy. He said he'd prefer money. He went to get the checkbook and he brought it out to me. I was going to grab his leg and get him down on the ground and wallop him, but he tossed me the checkbook and a pen and told me to write it out for six thousand dollars. And I would've done it, but just then the wolf came around the garage and sat down and looked at me. I told Rocky to go in the house and get the gun. And then I thought better of it. I told him to go get the package of sirloins out of the freezer. So he did. He tossed it to the wolf. The wolf tried to chew his way into it, but it was hard as a board. And there I lay, all fresh and meaty. Luckily, Sandy came home right at that moment. She ran the wolf off with a rake and then she told me that four thousand dollars would be enough for her, so I wrote out the check and the ambulance came and I was in the hospital for three weeks, and the leg's been fine, except it throbs whenever a storm is on the way."

James asked why Oscar was trapping for wolves and he said there had been a wolf who frightened some children and was coming too close to town, and Faye and James glanced at each other.

They sat chewing their food thoughtfully and Liz said, "I never heard that story before."

Oscar said, "That's because I never told it before."

"Where is Rocky now?" said Faye.

Oscar didn't know. They hadn't heard from him since he got out of the navy and got a job in New York driving a double-decker London omnibus.

"I remember waiting for the school bus when I was a kid," said James. He was about to launch into a story about that, while circling behind Leo—it was a story involving a pump handle and he would pick up an andiron from the fireplace to demonstrate how he almost put his tongue on the handle and he'd angle behind Leo and yank his right shoe off. He had thought of braining him with the andiron, but that would be too big a shock for his uncle. But then Uncle Earl cut him off and jumped in to talk about the winter of 1931. "There never was a winter like it. Snow blew into big drifts a hundred feet high, like mountains, and though it was only ten miles to school, they sent Mr. Turner to pick us up in his sleigh. He wore a big fur cap and had eyebrows the size of Norwegian rats and a big handlebar mustache, and he drove a team of black horses pulling a sleigh with a bearskin rug with the head of the bear still attached and us young 'uns dove under the bearskin and Mr. Turner cracked the whip and off we went to school. We crossed the river over the ice and rode through the swamp and were attacked there by ragged men in gray who leaped out from behind stumps, the last desperate remnants of the Army of Northern Virginia looking for little Yankee children to kidnap for ransom in hopes of raising money to buy gunpowder from the Canadians and put the Confederacy together again. Old men in gray waving their rifles and whooping and yelling, and we had to race away across the frozen tundra and get to school, which was held in a cave back then. You crawled in through a long narrow hole to a cavern, where you could stand up, and there were flaming torches set in iron brackets in the stones, and deep down below the earth there was an enormous room heated by hot springs that bubbled up in a pool, and dazzling bright because the walls were quartz and jasper and mica, which reflected the lantern light and made it feel like sunlight, and acres of precious stones lying loose all around, and we sat down at our desks feeling warm and happy, and I don't know where our teachers came from—children didn't ask so many questions back then; we were brought up to accept things as they were and be grateful and not ask why—but they were very beautiful women with long golden hair in soft tendrils who circulated among us singing in low voices, and their feet were bare and did not quite touch the ground. We were so grateful to be safe from the blizzard, we did our lessons faithfully and learned how to spell, which children today who grow up with reliable electrical power, and computers, never learn. Their spelling is atrocious. No reason not to love them, of course. They are wonderful kids. But I just wonder sometimes."

Twelve people around the long table, and out came a crock of fish soup redolent of onion and garlic and platters of pork and potatoes and a boatload of gravy, and Uncle Earl arose to say grace, holding his internal organs in his hand. "This is my last Christmas, Lord, and I am fully grateful for it. Thank you for bringing me this far. I ask no more. Thank you for Rosana and thanks to Jefferson County for the generosity. And thank you, Lord, for this brief time of peace and contentment and everybody getting along. And now let's eat." Rosana stood in the doorway, dabbing at her eyes. "Dig in!" he hollered. They sat and chewed and the sheer butteriness of everything, the pork and gravy, the glitter of fat in the spuds, made them dozy, even the FBI agent. He did not seem to be watching James so closely. At one point Leo's eyes closed for a long moment. He appeared to be ripe for the picking. And then Liz, who had had three glasses of red wine, clinked on her glass and stood up and said, "I'm glad you're all having fun and I hope that in the midst of it all you stop to consider that this may well be our last Christmas in a free country unless people listen to the truth and take action against Obama and his plans for total subjugation. But I promised Leo I wasn't going to talk politics on Christmas Eve, so I won't, difficult though it be for a patriot who believes in our Constitution to remain silent in the face of a noncitizen president in the White House attempting to subvert our way of life. I want to thank you, Daddy, for making me feel good about myself and not have to be like everybody else. And when you're gone, I'm going to stay here in Looseleaf and build a community of people dedicated to freedom." And she plopped down.

Well, Faye was not about to let Liz hog the spotlight, so she popped right up and spread her hands out in a long, lingering, beneficent gesture, her eyes closed, and said, "This is a thank you to the force of love that watches over all of us now and at all times, without which we would be lost forever."

"Oh God," said Liz.

Faye was unfazed. "In the great Ojibway tradition and in the traditions of all of us in the storytelling community, this time of year is sacred because it is a time of going back to origins and first causes, and whether we tell the story of the Christ child come to earth in Bethlehem and surrounded by cattle and shepherds, or we tell the story of the Great White

Bear who led our ancestors over the ice bridge from Siberia and down into the New World, this is nonetheless a sacred time and a time when each of us can pause and recollect our own story of who we are and where we come from and in this way get a clearer visualization of our journey—"

Oscar dinged on his glass. "Excuse me, but your ancestors didn't come over on an ice bridge from Siberia. They came from England on a ship. You're English, same as us. You're not Ojibway."

"I was made Ojibway in a spirit healing ceremony on the Arizona desert six years ago," she said. "I was born again on the desert, holding the sacred yucca in my hands, smoking the sacred mesquite."

"You've been smoking too much mesquite, then," he said. "You're one of us, Faye. Indian you ain't."

"Don't limit other people, Oscar. I'm a wayfarer. I am not defined by some old stereotype you have of me."

"Not defining you, Faye. Just telling you who you are so you don't make a fool of yourself."

Leo was pouring himself another glass of wine. His fourth. A disciplined G-man would not be drinking at such a time, but Leo had been undercover so long he had lost his edge. He definitely looked sleepy.

Uncle Earl got to his feet and dinged on a glass for silence. "I just remembered more about 1931. I was just a kid. I knew we didn't have much money. Our clothes were thin and we ate bean soup twice a day and Mama paid the rent with the money I earned from my paper route, but nonetheless she wanted to have Christmas. She went to the store and bought a big orange for me and a book, *The Chilstrom Boys on the S.S. Araby*, about two farm boys who stow aboard a freighter for the South Seas and solve the robbery of a sacred jade. We had beeswax candles and she lit them and we waited for Dad to come home from the farm where he was hiring out to muck out the barn for an old lady. He had to walk five miles to get home and it was late when he arrived, all worn out and discouraged, and Mama waiting up for him with two cups of eggnog and a shot of bourbon and two cigarettes. They were staunch Methodists, but on Christmas Eve they made an exception. So they smoked a cigarette and sipped the eggnog, and she put on the radio, and a jazz band was playing, and she danced with him. But his heart wasn't in it. She put his hand on her thigh and tried to kiss him, but he turned away. My mother and dad standing on an old linoleum floor in candlelight and the old Atwater-Kent turned up and a man was singing about a cottage for two, and her trying to kiss him and him turning away. It broke her heart. They thought I was asleep, but I wasn't. She sat down and smoked that second cigarette alone, and he looked out the window. He said, 'We can't afford to have another baby now. Can't even afford the one we got.' And she said, 'I'm not talking about that.' And he said nothing, and she said, 'I'm taking Buddy and going to live with my sister in North Dakota.' And that's how I came here."

Rosana brought out bowls of walnuts and dates and a pitcher of eggnog with rum to flavor it, and Oscar sat down at the piano and banged out:

On the road to Mandalay
where the flying fishes play
and the dawn comes up like thunder
out of China cross the bay

and

Nita Juanita, tell my soul that we must part . . . Nita
Juanita, lead thou on, my heart.

They stood shoulder to shoulder behind Oscar, their voices mingling, and James stood next to Leo and put an arm around him. Leo was drunk. They sang about coming with all the faithful upon a midnight clear to see the radiant streams from Thy holy face. And then Uncle Earl started singing "Silent Night" and Faye turned out the lights and the candles flickered, the fragrance of pine in the air, and coffee and saffron, and outside the snow was falling and James, who hadn't cried real tears since last Christmas, could feel them coming around again.

Everyone was in a mellow mood, even Liz.

Uncle Earl opened up a fresh bottle of brandy. "Clean glasses!" he said to Faye, and she jumped up and got a box of Dixie cups. "Glasses!" he said. "The good ones!" So she rustled up the family heirloom Waterford crystal goblets and washed the dust off and Earl poured a couple fingers of brandy in each and swished some around in his mouth and leaned back and closed his eyes. James stood in front of him, a camera in hand, and shot pictures of the old man, his eyes closed, as any storyteller's are when he's delving deep into memory.

"I remember the year I went up to Alaska to drive truck when they were building the Alcan Highway, and I stuck around in November to go bear hunting with some Eskimos I met in a bar in Fairbanks, and that was the year a storm came through on Armistice Day and dumped about six feet of snow. Well, we just stayed with the truck and got out okay, but we heard about a mining camp just south of there—they hadn't gotten their provisions in, and when two weeks passed and no help arrived, they looked around at each other and made some difficult choices. They scratched off the bonier ones—too hard to clean—and they marked a couple of the fat ones for harvesting. And of course the fat men knew it, even though the others tried to pretend it wasn't happening. And late at night, after devotions, the two fat men made their escape. They snuck out and put on their snowshoes and

headed for the highway. Two great big guys. One was the
camp cook and the other was the dynamiter who set off the
charges in the mineshaft when they needed to go deeper.
Well, being hefty men and no athletes, they got winded after a couple thousand yards, and the alarm bell rang, and the
camp organized a rescue party to go find them. A hunting
party, I should say. The moon was full and the fat men's trail
was easy to follow, the way they thrashed around in the
snow, and the hunters spotted them making their way
around the south face of Golden Girl Mountain and saw how
slow they were moving. So the hunters circled down to the
lower slopes to intercept them at a line of aspen trees. They'd
shoot both of them right there, gut them, skin them, butcher
the meat, and pack it out on a toboggan. Easy pickings. They
hid in the aspens, licking their chops, waiting for dinner to
arrive, and then they saw a flash of flame. They knew what
it was and tried to run, but the snow was too deep. The
dynamiter had set off a charge and started the biggest avalanche you ever saw. Half the mountain came sliding down,
and the two fat men rode down on it, paddling and kicking
like crazy to stay afloat, and the hungry men in the aspen
trees were never seen again. The fat men rode the snow for
six miles all the way down to the Matanuska Valley and slid
up to the highway just as a bus came along. It stopped. On
the bus were fifteen attractive young ladies who were part
of an evangelism crusade and ten lumberjacks who thought

they'd died and gone to heaven. Fifteen women for ten men seemed like the right ratio to them, and of course the ladies were all born-again Christians, but—if only the bus would get stuck and all of them be snowbound for a week or two or three, the lumberjacks figured that human nature would take its course and the pleasure urge would prevail. And then these two fatsos climb aboard all snowy and wet, and that promised to screw everything up. The lumberjacks bided their time until the bus came to a snowslide and stopped. It was twilight. The lumberjacks got out shovels to dig, and the dynamiter spoke up nice and pert and said, "Hey, I know a better way!" So he prepared a charge of dynamite. A couple big red sticks tied together and a long fuse, and he got it all rigged up, the lumberjacks hoping he'd set it off accidentally and blow himself sky-high, and he laid it in the deepest part of the snowbank and hollered 'Fire in the hole!' and all the lumberjacks dashed for cover. But while the charge was being rigged, the cook had gone around and let air out of the bus tires, and so he and the dynamiter jumped on board the bus with the girls and drove right over the snowslide. And when the lumberjacks gave chase, the dynamite went off and the lumberjacks slid into a deep crevasse and it took ten days to rescue them, by which time they'd gone berserk and were babbling and pulling out their hair by the fistful. Two men with fifteen young women who were praising God for their deliverance. The cook and the dynamiter had a day and a half to get to know the girls, and when they got to Anchorage each of them had found a wife, and of course they had to go to church and get saved, but that was a small price to pay for the love of a beautiful woman."

James got engrossed in the story and forgot about Leo, and then Leo stood up and dinged on a glass.

"This is the fifteenth Christmas I've spent with all of you here in Looseleaf and I want to thank you for all these wonderful stories of bygone days of yesteryear, and now I have a little story of my own. But not so sweet."

Liz looked at him thoughtfully. James edged around behind the tree. Leo didn't notice.

"Next week I am moving to Washington, D.C., to take up a new position in the antiterrorism office of the FBI." He reached into his pocket and pulled out the badge. "My name isn't Wimmer, it's Krainis. Lawrence B. Krainis, Special Agent. I've been here undercover, and now my job is done." He turned to Liz. "I just want you to know, from the heart, that you were everything I ever wanted in a wife. It's not about you at all."

Liz did not seem fazed whatsoever. "If it's the Possum Comatosis you're after, G-Man, you're a day late and a dollar short."

"My colleagues will round them up, Liz."

"No, they won't, G-Man. I knew somebody was watching us because I can sense satellite waves, and so I moved the Freedom Center out of the power plant a month ago. Put them on a truck and wished them well, and I have no idea where they went. But somewhere in America, they're working to reestablish the Constitution of the United States of America. You can count on that big time."

Leo—or Lawrence B. Krainis—shrugged. "We'll see about that."

"You've got nothing on me, G-Man."

It appeared to James that Leo was standing on his left foot, ready to raise the right and fire. He tried to get around Oscar so he could grab Leo, and then Faye got in the way and leaned over and grabbed a carving knife from beside the meat platter.

"If this is about the sacred medicinal plants of the Ojibway, you've bitten off more than you can chew, white man. I may talk like a hophead, but I could put this knife between your ribs as easy as I could filet a walleye, maybe easier."

"Your drug habits don't interest me, Faye, and they're of no interest to the government. But Liz is going to have to come with me."

James stepped forward and faced him just like he'd faced the wolf. "You're barking in the wrong culvert, Mr. Krainis. It's Christmas, and you're a guest here. And no longer a welcome one."

"There's no holiday where crime fighting is concerned," Leo said. He walked slowly around the table, hopping on his left foot, his eyes flitting from side to side lest anyone should attempt a sudden move. Oscar was on his feet, and Rosana had come into the room holding a whisk. "Nobody move so much as an eyebrow or my roscoe's gonna start talking," he said. "I've taken as much of your guff as I'm going to take. Fifteen years I've been married to a felon as I gathered evidence of her perfidy. Talk about sacrifices! I gave fifteen years of my life in North Dakota so I could bust up a terrorist ring. I gave up fine restaurants, movies, concerts, the ballet, theater, so I could live in Nowheresville and capture an outlaw. And I'm not about to let you people talk me out of it." As he spoke, he sidled around Uncle Earl's chair, keeping his eye on James, not watching where he was stepping, and he stepped onto the plastic bag containing the liver and the pancreas. The old man let out a bloodcurdling shriek, and the FBI man jumped back and tripped on a lamp cord and fell like a bucket of bricks, and James leaped forward and pulled off Leo's right shoe containing the gun and pointed it at Leo's head. "One burp out of you, Judas, and you're going to find out more than you wanted to know about the afterlife."

Uncle Earl clutched his abdomen. "I'm leaving!" he yelled. "I'm out of here! I got only seconds to live! Better come give me a hug right now and don't wait. The shades of night are falling fast! The curfew bell is a-ringing! I can hear them calling! It's the moaning of the bar! Heading out to sea! O yes—the end is nigh!"

Liz knelt down by his side and Faye grabbed him, as Leo stood up. He leered at James. "Fell for the old shoe pistol trick," he said, and twisted his right hand, and suddenly a revolver jumped out of his shirt cuff and into his palm. He backed toward the door. "No sudden moves," he said. "Or I'll make this a Christmas you'll remember for a long time to come." Just as an old gray-haired lady in a black silk dress and a veil stepped smartly into the room and pulled out a pump handle and swung it and hit him right in the elbow, in that tender spot that everyone knows so well, and he dropped the revolver and grabbed his elbow and jumped up and down in pain, crying out *Oh oh oh oh oh oh oh*. His long training as an FBI agent had not prepared him for the vulnerability of this particular bone.

Uncle Earl laughed to see it. Despite his bruised organs, the sight of the agent dancing in pain and emitting high-pitched squeals amused him, and he chortled and slapped his thigh. He said, "You were the most boring son-in-law a man could have, Leo, but I see you had terpsichorean talent we hadn't known about. And now I'd be obliged if you'd just get in your car and drive away."

"Can't drive away. We're snowbound," said Oscar.

The old woman in the doorway said, "You're not snow-bound anymore." It was Joyce, dressed up as Mrs. Manicotti. She looked at James and gestured with her thumb. "You," she said. "Come with me."

She led him to the door and put his parka over his shoulders and out the door they went, and there sat her snowmobile, idling, and she climbed on and he climbed on behind her and she gunned the engine with a tremendous roar and headed across the fields toward Bismarck. "Where did you come from?" James said, but she didn't hear him over the engine's roar. "I heard you're pregnant," he yelled into her ear, but she didn't hear that, either.

She threw away the gray wig as she raced toward the flashing beacon light atop the North Dakota State Capitol in downtown Bismarck, and nothing more was said until she brought the machine to a stop in front of the Hotel Roland and turned off the engine.

"I have news," she said.

"I figured it out," he said.

"I'm expecting a baby."

"That's wonderful."

"You're not upset?"

"I'm happy as I can be."

He started to thank her for coming to his rescue, and she shushed him and led him into the simple splendor of the hotel and up to their suite on the fourth floor, where she hung a NOT NOW sign on the knob and closed the door, and it remained closed for more than an hour.

They emerged around eight that evening and went for a walk under the streetlights, the stars in the sky more or less as you see on Christmas cards, nebulae spiraling in the chill pristine beauty of the world of stillness. Shimmery flakes fell through the air. A lovely night, the lights of Christmas trees in houses, snowy branches on the bare trees, no traffic on the snowy streets and then a team of big-rumped caramel-colored horses with jingle bells on their harnesses came trotting along pulling a hay wagon piled with families singing "Jingle Bells." The yards lay under undulating swells of snow, strings of little white lights twinkling on trees and buildings all over town. And up the street some kids hollered "Ho Ho Ho, WHO WOULDN'T GO!" Mr. Sparrow walked with his arm around his wife's waist and the tips of his fingers brushing her belly, inside of which slept his child, so newly formed it was neither boy nor girl yet, just a seed pushing toward completion.

"I saw a notice for a Living Nativity tonight at a church down this way," said Mrs. Sparrow. "We could be shepherds. You just throw on a robe and hold a shepherd's crook and that's it."

"How about I be a spectator?"

"Well, the shepherds *were* spectators."

He was not sure he was into group adoration right then, but they pressed forward down the street and past an old saggy house at the end of the block lit up like a casino, with flashing blue lights, green zipper lights, Santa in his sleigh atop the roof and Rudolph's nose flashing, Frosty in the yard with the Wise Men, Tiny Tim, Winnie the Pooh, the Grinch, Dorothy and Toto, Jimmy Stewart, and past little houses like his in Looseleaf, and found Holy Redeemer Lutheran Church, where a crowd had gathered around a manger in the parking lot and a woman in a white cassock and silvery cape smiled at them and welcomed them.

"If there are sheep here, I'm allergic to wool," said Mr. Sparrow.

"We don't use sheep anymore. We use dogs and we put sheep's clothing on them, but it's not wool, it's synthetic."

"I could be a wise man."

"Already got three of them. Come be a shepherd."

So the two of them donned robes and stood, holding shepherd's crooks as the moon shone down and lit up the yard like a circus ring, and there by the manger with a Christmas star on the roof they stood by the Holy Infant in the hay as children dressed in sparkly angel gowns sang something in Latin and the Magi parked themselves in majestic humility the night before Christmas. Not far away, people rushed through the malls in desperate need of a few more gifts, but there in the snowy parking lot a sweet, simple devotion rose in their midst and the shepherds looked around them with delicate feeling and thought better of each other than they would have otherwise. It was Christmas. He was a boy in buckle overshoes walking home through the snow, and he was the young man in the choir looking at the words *Hodie Christus natus est* as Mrs. Peterson tapped her pencil on the music stand, and he was the husband of Joyce and the father of their child in waiting. And he was a shepherd, one of the lucky ones to whom the Lord was revealed. The cold air in his nostrils was thrilling and the stillness of the street and the stucco bungalows and the snowy yards and the serene stillness of the muffled crowd gathered around the manger, all at attention, like hunters, waiting for something, and maybe keen attention was the point of it. To be awake and alert and to open your heart to accept the miracle.

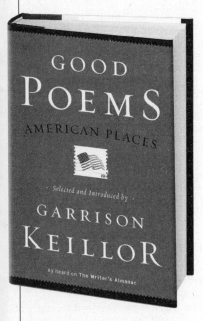

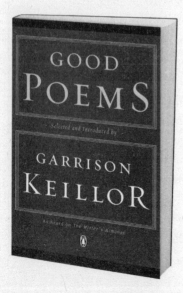

MORE FROM GARRISON KEILLOR

Pilgrims

Lake Wobegon goes to Italy to decorate a war hero's grave, led by Marjorie Krebsbach, with radio host Gary Keillor along for the ride.

ISBN 978-0-14-311785-8

Liberty

The Chairman of the Fourth of July, Clint Bunsen, is in the midst of an identity crisis brought on by a DNA test just as he turns sixty.

ISBN 978-0-14-311611-0

Pontoon

As the wedding of the decade approaches (accompanied by wheels of imported cheese and giant shrimp shish kebabs), the good, loving people of Lake Wobegon do what they do best: drive each other slightly crazy.

ISBN 978-0-14-311410-9

PENGUIN BOOKS

MORE FROM GARRISON KEILLOR

The Book of Guys
ISBN 978-0-14-023372-8

Leaving Home
ISBN 978-0-14-013160-4

Lake Wobegon Days
ISBN 978-0-14-013161-1

Love Me
ISBN 978-0-14-200499-9

Lake Wobegon Summer 1956
ISBN 978-0-14-200093-9

Wobegon Boy
ISBN 978-0-14-027478-3

PENGUIN BOOKS